The YouthPower Guide

How to Make Your Community Better

A Manual Based on the Work of the **YouthPower Project** of **El Arco Iris Youth and Community Arts Center**
A Program of
Nueva Esperanza, Inc.
Holyoke, Massachusetts

by
Urban Places Project
University of Massachusetts, Amherst
2000

The YouthPower Guide Project Team

YouthPower (A Project of El Arco Iris Youth and Community Arts Center)

Jose Colon, Co-Director
Imre Kepes, Co-Director
Luz Ivette Cruz, Staff
Kelley Brown, Amherst College Intern
Raul Bermudez, Peer Leader
Anthony Bermudez, Peer Leader
Nelson Bolorin, Peer Leader
Johanna Collazo, Peer Leader
Marisella Diaz, Peer Leader
Yarily Santana, Peer Leader

Urban Places Project

Ann Forsyth, Co-Director
Henry Lu, Co-Director
Patricia McGirr, Co-Director
Mark Fisher
Mihaela Zaharescu

Acknowledgments

This report was funded through a grant from the Boston Foundation for Architecture and based on the work of YouthPower, an After-School Community Service Learning Project funded by a Massachusetts Department of Education Community Service Learning Program grant from the Massachusetts Service Alliance. This material is based upon work supported by the Massachusetts Service Alliance. Opinions or points of view expressed in this document are those of the authors and do not necessarily reflect the official position of the Alliance.

Additional funding provided by the Massachusetts Chapter of the American Planning Association.

Additional support provided by UMass Extension, University of Massachusetts, Amherst, Massachusetts, United States Department of Agriculture cooperating. UMass Extension provides equal opportunity in programs and employment.

Thanks to: Jim Morrissey, Greater Holyoke, Inc. and John Linehan, Nueva Esperanza, Inc.

Published by UMass Extension, University of Massachusetts, Amherst, Massachusetts.
ISBN 1-892893-01-0

Contents

Contents, continued

INTRODUCTION

THE PURPOSE OF THIS MANUAL AND HOW YOU CAN USE IT

Introduction

THE REASON FOR THIS MANUAL

Have you ever wanted to make your community better: build a park, paint a mural, or create a walkway along a river? Then keep reading on.

The manual is written to be used by young people aged 10 to 19, and by people who work with these young people. It contains ideas that will help anyone who wants to change their neighborhood for the better, whether doing just one activity, or making a plan for the whole neighborhood.

WHAT IS IN THE MANUAL

Since 1995, El Arco Iris and YouthPower have worked on projects involving young people in planning and building a better neighborhood. This manual describes many of the groups' most successful activities and explains how you can use them to make a plan for your neighborhood and to do projects that improve your neighborhood.

The manual is in two parts.

- In the first and main part of the manual — Build Your Team! Dream It! Plan It! Do it! — we describe twenty-four activities. In each case we say **what** the activity is about and explain **how** you do the activity. Some activities also have a part called **why** that explains the purpose of the activity, and others give **examples** of the activity. Each activity is designed to last 60 to 75 minutes. Some activities may require more than one session to complete.
- The second part of the manual gives more detailed instructions for peer leaders and youth supervisors.

HOW TO USE THE MANUAL

The manual is designed to provide a basic framework and steps to follow, based on what we found to work. Groups are encouraged to be creative and to modify the framework and steps to meet their community needs.

Groups that are not interested in making a neighborhood plan, but just want to do a project, can use the Do It! section and skip the Dream It! and Plan It! sections.

A NOTE ON COPYRIGHT

El Arco Iris Youth and Community Arts Center
60 Hamilton Street
Holyoke, MA 01040, USA
413 532 2360, fax 413 533 8360.

To order additional copies of this book contact the:

UMass Extension Bookstore
Draper Hall, Box 32010
Amherst, MA 01003-2010.
413 545 2717 or
toll-free within Massachusetts:1-877-UMASSXT.
Fax: 413 545 5174.
Visit us on the Web at
www.umass.edu/umext/bookstore.

SECTION ONE

Deciding on your purpose

MAKING THE COMMITMENT TO IMPROVE YOUR COMMUNITY

ACTIVITY 1

1.Deciding on your purpose

WHAT

As a team you need to decide on what you will do. In this activity you come up with a mission statement that gives the project a name and says what the team is going to do.

MISSION STATEMENT EXAMPLE

The AZZ Club Team will design and build a better mousetrap so that more mice are caught without being hurt (the mice that is).

Things you need:

- Big sheets of newsprint paper
- Thick colored markers

HOW

Make a mission statement and a contract

✷ The team first needs to decide if they will do a short-term **project,** or make a **plan** for the whole neighborhood and do several projects.

- A **project** is a short-term activity focused on getting a specific thing done. Examples include cleaning up a park, repainting a building, or making a mural.
- A neighborhood **plan** is long-term and more complicated, and provides an overall vision for an area like a neighborhood. To carry out a plan requires working with other groups and doing several projects over a long period of time. It requires a long-term commitment.

✷ **A mission statement is a short statement of what you will do, why you will do it, and how**. It can be one or two sentences long. To decide on a mission statement use brainstorming and discussions (see instructions on opposite page).

- The team decides on a contract that says how they will commit to the project and everyone signs it.
- The team also decides on a name for the project.

✷ You can also start out by doing a short-term project, then decide you want to do a neighborhood plan later.

END PRODUCT: A mission statement and a contract.

BASIC RULES OF BRAINSTORMING

- Brainstorming aims to generate ideas rather than make decisions.
- Everyone should speak.
- All ideas should be written down.
- Ideas should not be debated. The evaluation step comes later.
- Creative, unusual, and "impractical" ideas are valuable and should be written down.
- Keep the discussion going and do not let anyone dominate the discussion.
- After the first rush of ideas, suggestions usually quiet down for a while. Do not stop the session here as the best ideas usually come after this quiet period.

BRAINSTORMING ROLES

- The **brainstorm leader** asks questions, keeps people on time, and makes sure everyone speaks. This role can be taken by a member of the group or by an adult.
- A **recorder** writes down the ideas. The writing should be big enough for everyone to see.

Working as a team

ACTIVITY 2

2. Working as a team

WHAT

This activity helps you learn how to work as a team.

HOW

✷ Brainstorm rules for your team.

See Basic Rules of Brainstorming in Activity 1.

- Brainstorm to decide what kind of rules you want for your team.
- Write the rules on a large piece of white cardboard.

Things you need:
- Big sheets of newsprint
- Large felt tip markers
- Big sheets of white cardboard

✷ Learn how to run meetings.

- Learn how to make **an agenda** for meetings — the agenda should show what you are going to talk about in the meeting, how long each "agenda item" should take, and who will be in charge of what parts of the meeting.
- Meetings should start with a brief review of rules, then someone should explain what the purpose of the meeting is and what will be done in the meeting. It is good to have a break or an energizer activity about half way through the meeting. It is good to include activities in the meeting so everyone can participate. Have a brief evaluation at the end to get feedback.

WHAT IS A PEER LEADER?

A peer leader is an older youth participant who acts as a role model and helps to plan and lead meetings.

✷ Build leadership.

- You should select young people with experience in groups to be peer leaders. Each peer leader gets a turn leading meetings. It is a good idea to work in pairs.

✷ **Build your team.**

- Give "jobs" to all the peer leaders such as leading the meetings, writing the agenda, recording ideas at meetings, keeping track of time, and making sure rules are followed. Also let other younger participants help by writing, keeping time, and doing simpler jobs.
- Regularly talk about how well or not well things are going (be honest). Talk about how you could make things better.

END PRODUCT: People who know how to work in a team.

SAMPLE AGENDA FORM

TIME	WHO	WHAT	NOTES
5 min.		INTRODUCTION • rules • what this meeting is about	
35 min.		MAIN AGENDA ITEMS: • planning a project • what needs to be done • who will do what • what do we need to do the project?	
10 min.		ENERGIZER • game	
20 min.		PLAN FOR NEXT MEETING • what should we do next? • what do we need to plan on next meeting?	
10 min.		EVALUATION • what went well in the meeting? • what didn't you like and how would you make it better?	

BUILD YOUR TEAM!

Outreach to other young people

ACTIVITY 3

3. Outreach to other young people

WHAT

It is often useful to work with other young people as projects progress, or when trying to undertake large or long-term projects or plans. This involves bringing new young people into one's own group.

HOW

✸ **Prepare for doing outreach.**

- Make flyers describing your project with the name of the project.
- Practice doing outreach with each other by having one person be the outreach person and the other a youth in the community.

✸ **Recruit for your program.**

- Go door to door and to other community groups to recruit for your program.
- Invite young people from your community and other youth organizations to come to a presentation and question and answer session.
- Questions you could ask at your presention are listed in the box on the opposite page.

END PRODUCT: A larger team to work on projects or plans.

QUESTION AND ANSWER SESSION

Questions you can ask include:

- **Are there things you would like to make better in your neighborhood?**
- **Do you think young people can make a difference?**
- **Do you feel that you can really make your neighborhood better and would you like to be part of trying that?**

Make flyers describing your project and distribute them to other young people.

DREAM IT!

Brainstorming a vision of your ideal community !

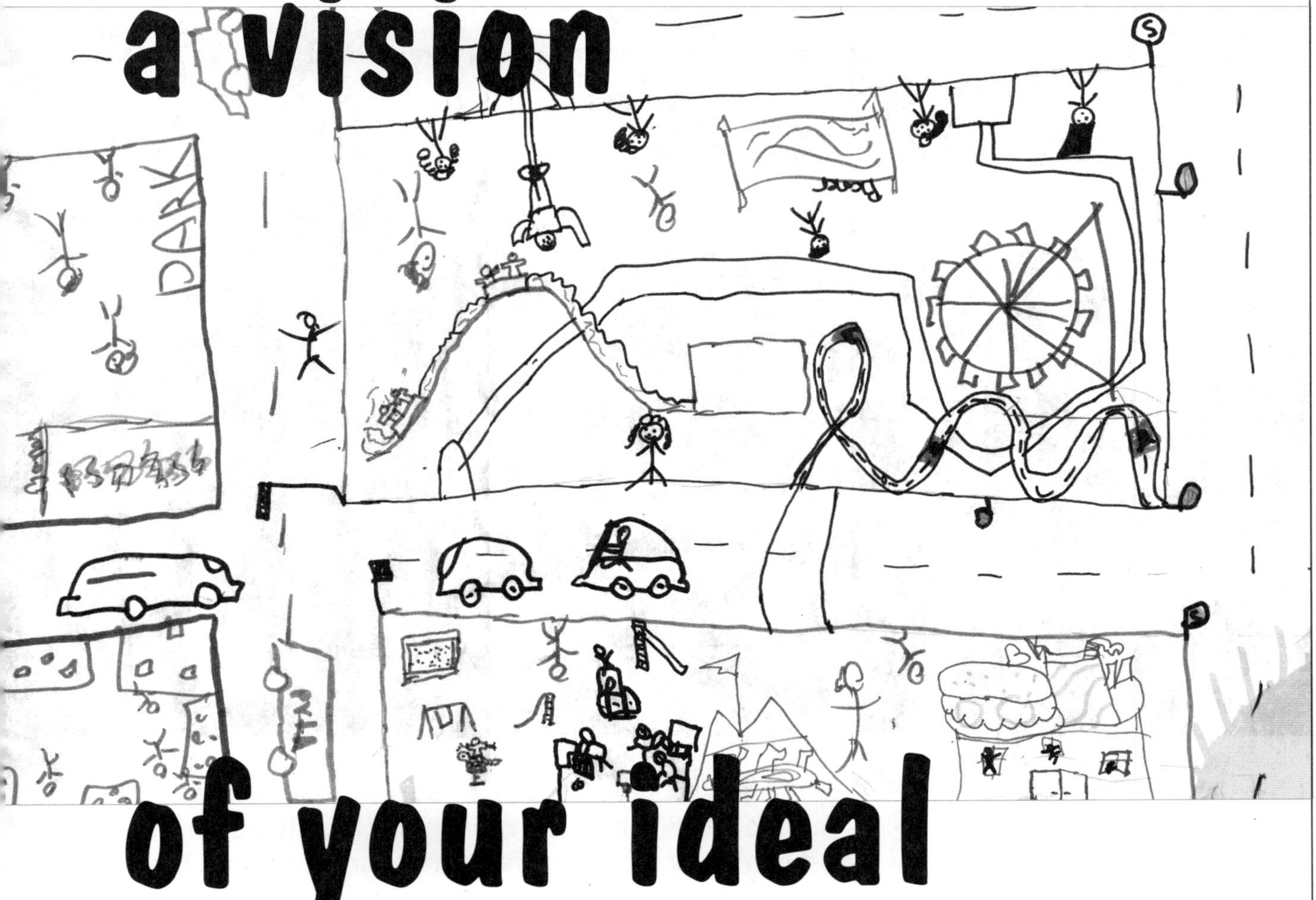

ACTIVITY 4

4. Brainstorming a vision of your ideal community

WHAT

Create a picture of your ideal community.

See Basic Rules of Brainstorming in Activity 1.

HOW

Brainstorm your ideas for your ideal neighborhood.

(See rules for brainstorming in Activity 1.)

- A peer leader leads the group in brainstorming ideas.
- Someone writes ideas on the flip chart or large piece of paper.

> Things you need:
> - A flip chart and BIG sheets of paper at least 3'x4'. (You can tape sheets together.)
> - Large felt tip markers
> - OPTIONAL: Large sheets of cardboard or foam core board to paste drawings on

Draw a picture of your ideal community.

- Divide your group into teams of no more than 6 people.
- Each group decides for itself how they want to draw their map. Everyone must participate. You can draw pictures, use words, or symbols. Think of all the things you would want in your ideal community.

Present your picture.

- Each group then presents their vision map. Two people from each team are chosen to present the map. They say what is in the map and why it's there.

EXAMPLE OF AN IDEAL NEIGHBORHOOD

WHY

✷ **The whole group discusses what they learned.**

- What do you think are the best ideas for your community — why?
- What did you learn?
- How was it working as a team and presenting your ideas — what did you learn from that?

END PRODUCT: A picture showing your ideal neighborhood.

How do you experience your community ?

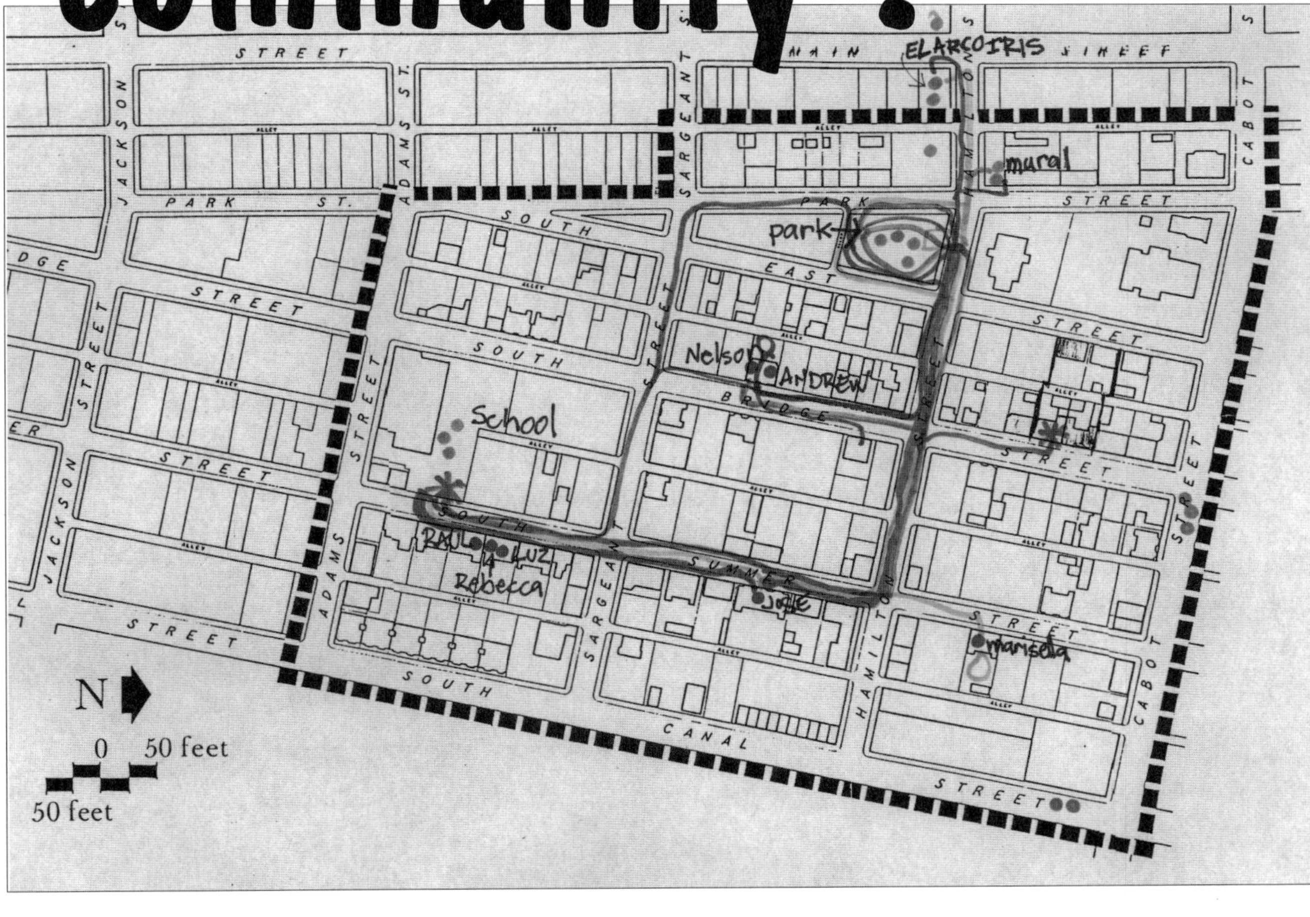

ACTIVITY 5

5. How do you experience your community?

WHAT

This activity helps you see how you experience your neighborhood. It lets you show where you live, where you go, and where you avoid going.

The exercise also allows you to become familiar with a map of your neighborhood and where things are.

It helps you see both the problems and the good things in your community.

HOW

✸ **Divide into groups of 4 to 6** sitting at a table with the map in the middle.

✸ **Have each person put dots on the map.**

♦ Put a red dot where you live and write your name beside it.

♦ Place green dots on the locations where you go or hang out and label them.

♦ Place yellow dots on landmarks and important places and label them.

♦ Place blue dots on the places you avoid and also give them labels.

♦ Draw lines to show paths you take through and around the neighborhood.

✸ **Each group presents their map.**

♦ The groups tell about the places they like and why, and the places they don't like and why.

END PRODUCT: A map on a board showing problems and opportunities.

Things you need:

- A large map of the neighborhood, at least 3 feet long, with enough copies so there is one between four to six participants. One of the departments at City Hall will probably have a good map: try calling planning or engineering. If they don't have one you can use a map blown up from a street directory
- Colored markers
- Stick-on dots and stars in red, green, yellow, and blue
- Thick corrugated cardboard or foam core board to paste the map on

Divide into groups of 4 to 6 people with a map in the middle of the table.

PLAN IT!

PLAN IT!

Neighborhood tour

WHAT'S GOOD AND WHAT NEEDS TO BE IMPROVED

ACTIVITY 6

6. Neighborhood tour

WHAT

Walking around your neighborhood is a good way to get to know what's in your neighborhood and to record places that need improvement and places that are good.

HOW

You can do one or more of the following activities.

Things you need:

- A stiff board like a 4' by 3' piece of corrugated card-board
- Glue sticks or scotch tape

And one or more of the following:

- Notepads and markers and a small map of the neighborhood
- A camera such as a Polaroid instant camera
- A video camera

✷ **Walk around the neighborhood with a notepad and small map** of the neighbor-hood.

- Write about sites — their problems and good things.
- Write about your ideas to make these places better.

✷ **Take pictures of areas or sites that are good and bad in the neighborhood**.

- Take a picture of the whole area or site.
- Take some close-up pictures of what is good and bad about each area.

✷ **Walk around the neighborhood with a video camera**.

- Take a shot that shows the specific area or site, and the environment around the site.
- Take some shots of good and bad things about the site.
- Take shots of your group reading their ideas about how to make the site better.

END PRODUCT: A map, photos, or videotape describing the good and bad parts of the neighborhood.

WHAT IS A SITE?

Site is a word used by architects, landscape architects, and planners to refer to a particular place or location.

NEIGHBORHOOD TOUR USING A NOTEPAD

PLAN IT!

Making a map

Of what's good and what's bad in your community

ACTIVITY 7

7. Making a map of what's good and what's bad in your community

WHAT

This activity is about making a map of the good and bad parts of your community that you found on your neighborhood tour.

HOW

✷ **Take your map of the neighborhood and draw lines around all the sites you identified on the neighborhood tour.**

- Number each site.

✷ **Tape lists of what is good and bad about each site near their location on the map.**

- You can use a photocopier to make the lists smaller (so they can fit on the map).

✷ **If you took pictures you can tape them next to the lists of good and bad things about each site.**

Things you need:

- A large map of your neighborhood taped to a much larger piece of white card-board or 1/4 inch plywood
- Scotch tape
- Pencils or pens
- Glue stick

WHAT'S BAD:
Trash

WHAT'S GOOD:
Mural

✷ **You can move the lists and pictures around until the map looks just right.**

- Glue the lists and pictures to the map.
- Finally, draw lines from the lists and pictures to the site each one is for.

END PRODUCT: Map of sites in the neighborhood.

PLAN IT!

Coming up with ideas to improve your community

ACTIVITY 8

PLAN IT!

8. Coming up with ideas to improve your community

WHAT

This activity is about coming up with a list of ideas to improve your community.

HOW

✸ Brainstorm what kinds of places and activities are important for a healthy community and what kinds of people live in the community.

- Make a list on the flip chart of the kinds of places and activities you think should be in your neighborhood (examples are: businesses, places for recreation, places to socialize, quiet and beautiful places, places for art and culture, etc.).
- Make a list of the kinds of people in your community (examples are: young, old, families, different ethnic groups, homeless, etc.).
- Tape the lists on the wall so everyone can see them.

✸ Divide the group into teams of 4 to 6 people to brainstorm ideas for improving the neighborhood.

- Each team brainstorms to come up with ideas for each of the kinds of places and activities discussed above. For each idea they write what kind(s) of people it is for.
- Each team can use ideas from the ideal community map and from the neighborhood tour (the ideal community map(s) and ideas from the tour should also be displayed).
- Each team chooses two people to present their list of projects.
- The teams get prizes for most ideas, best ideas, best presentation, and most creative ideas.

END PRODUCT: Ideas about potential projects.

Things you need:

- Pad of newsprint paper or a flip chart
- Colored markers

See Activity 1: Basic Rules of Brainstorming

See Activity 4: Brainstorming a vision

See Activity 6: Neighborhood tour

See Activity 21: Celebrations and awards

PLAN IT!

SCORE CARD	
TEAM "A"	
	SCORE: 1=ok 2=good 3=great
most ideas	2
best ideas	2
most creative ideas	3
best presentation	3
GRAND TOTAL	10

SAMPLE SCORE CARD

for the competition to come up with and present ideas for improving your community.

- There should be at least three "judges," each with a score card for each team.
- The team with the most total number of points wins.

PLAN IT!

PLAN IT!

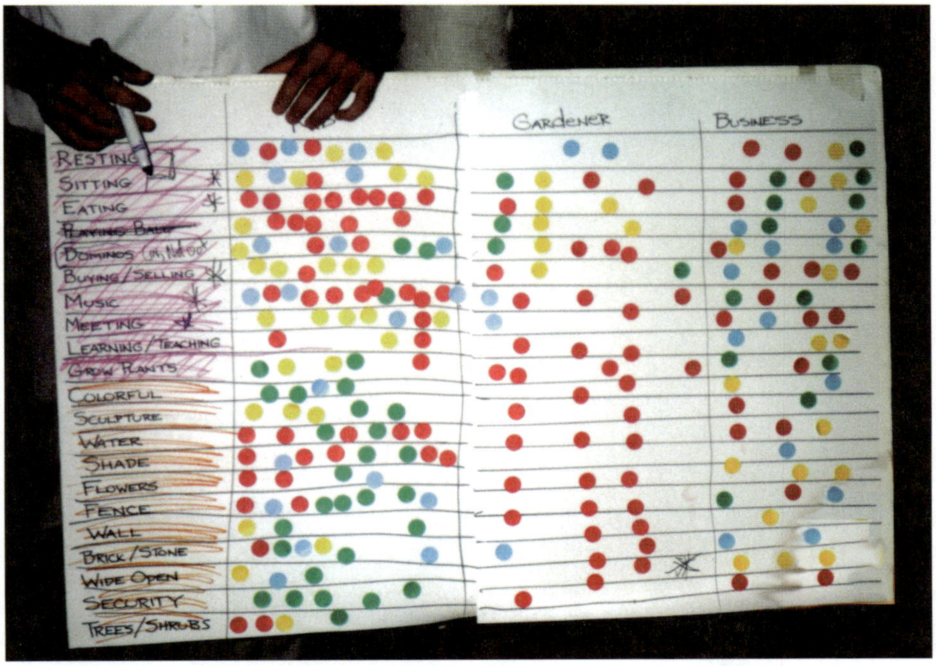

Choosing the best ideas

ACTIVITY 9

PLAN IT!

9. Choosing the best ideas

WHAT

This activity ranks the list of specific projects to determine what are the important issues and projects for your group to focus on.

Selection of projects is based on the goals of the team and factors such as learning potential, fun, and the value of the project to the community. This is decided jointly by the young people and the directors of the organization.

Things you need:

- Large sheets of newsprint paper
- Large colored markers
- Lots of colored dots for voting

HOW

✷ **Make a chart of your ideas.**

- Start with a list of projects generated in the earlier activities.
- Place the list of projects down the left side of the page, with a line under each one stretching across the whole sheet.
- Place the rating categories (listed below) across the top and draw a vertical line between each one. (This kind of diagram is called a matrix.)

RATING CATEGORIES MIGHT INCLUDE:

- **Fun**: Will this be fun for you and keep you interested?
- **Learning potential**: Are there opportunities for learning skills or concepts that will be beneficial to you?
- **Community service**: Will this project help the community?

✸ **Rank the projects by voting with stickers on the chart**. A good way to do this is to follow these steps.

- Give the different colors of stickers different meanings. (See the box for examples.)
- Give each person red, yellow, and green dots (or whatever colors you are using). They'll need as many dots as there are projects, times the number of rating categories; so, if there are 20 projects and three rating categories, they'll need 60 dots in all.

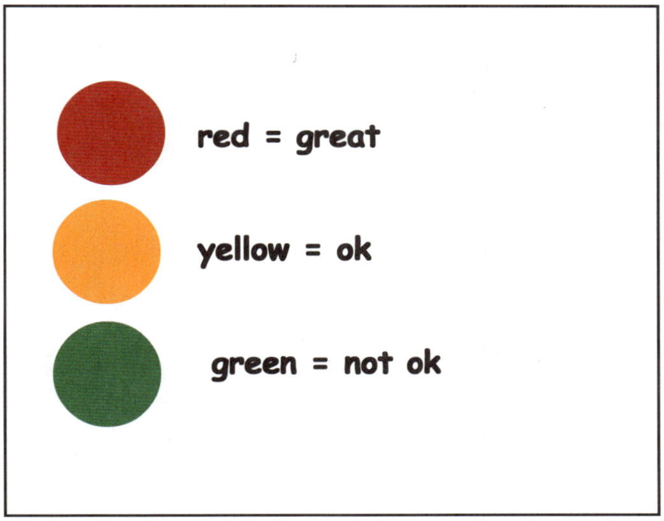

- Let people vote for each project in terms of each of the rating categories.
- If a project has all green dots in one category it should be cut out as it will not be fun, or not good for learning, or not have support.
- The remaining projects with the most red and yellow dots are the highest priority.
- Decide on the top four to seven projects.

END PRODUCT: A list of 4 to 7 potential projects.

PLAN IT!

PLAN IT!

Making a community map

OF YOUR IDEAS TO MAKE IT BETTER

ACTIVITY 10

10. Making a community map of your ideas to make it better

WHAT

You will draw pictures of your ideas to improve your neighborhood and put them on a map.

HOW

✷ **Each person chooses to draw at least one of the best ideas from the list of projects decided on in the last activity.**

✷ **Each person makes drawings of the ideas they chose and colors the drawings.**

- Each person writes what the idea is and why it is important.
- Each person presents their drawing(s) and says what it is and why it's important.

✷ **The whole group works together to decide where each idea should go on the map.**

✷ **Your group works together to tape the pictures on the map board next to the sites they go with.**

✷ **Draw lines from each picture to the sites they go with.**

You will need:

- A large map of your neighborhood with all the sites you looked at marked, and the whole thing should be mounted on a much larger piece of cardboard, white board (foamcore), or 1/4" plywood
- Paper and felt tip markers for drawing
- Scotch tape and/or glue sticks

END PRODUCT: Pictures of ideas to improve your neighborhood linked to their locations in the neighborhood.

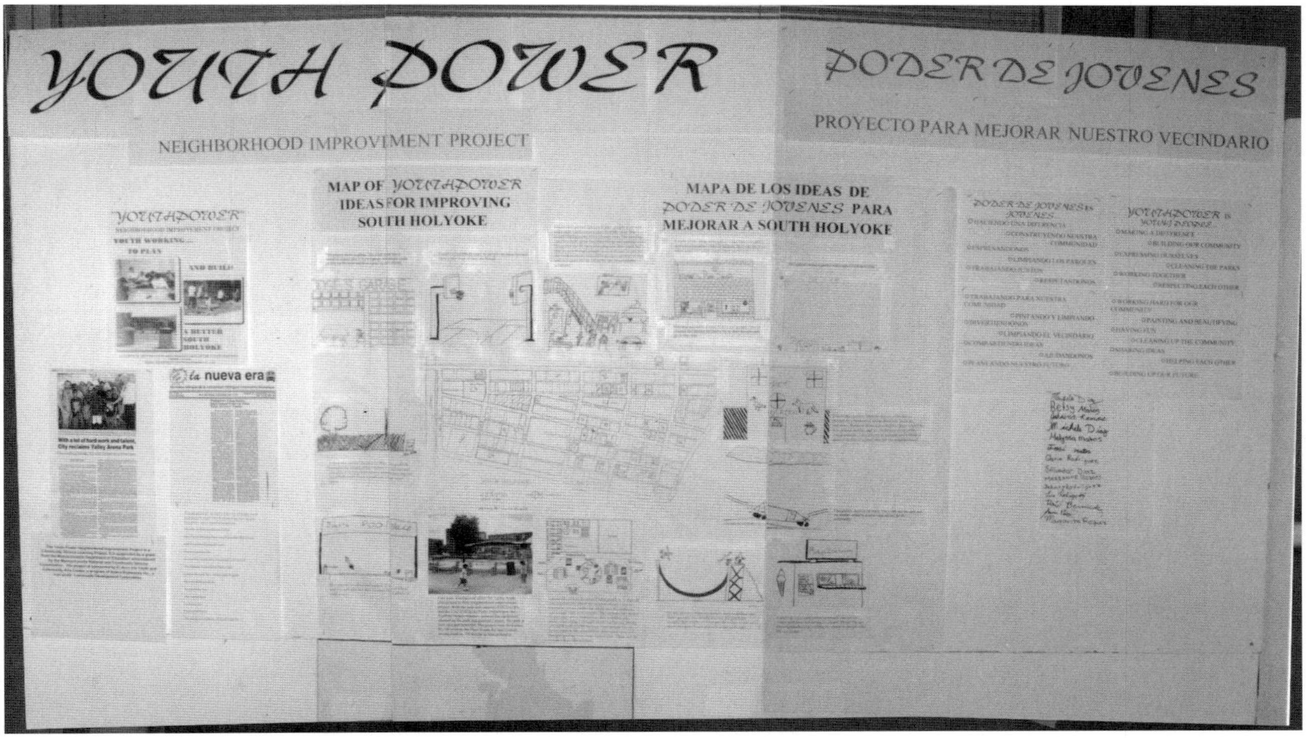

EXAMPLE OF COMMUNITY MAP

PLAN IT!

Getting community input and support

ACTIVITY 11

PLAN IT!

11. Getting community input and support

WHAT

This activity lets you find out how people in your community, other groups, and your town officials respond to your ideas, and what ideas they have.

HOW

✷ **Visit town officials and other groups to talk about your plan for your neighborhood.**

- Make an appointment to visit your planning board, community development office, parks department, conservation board, mayor, or selectboard.
- Show them your list of ideas and your community map. Get their input.

✷ **Present your neighborhood map and list of ideas to your community, other groups, and your town officials.**

- Plan for the meeting. Decide who will present the ideas on the map (it is best to chose two people to do this). Decide who will record the ideas from the community. Practice for the meeting.
- Make flyers for the meeting and mail them. Follow up with phone calls especially to other groups and to town officials to explain what you are doing.
- Present your map at the community meeting. Explain the map (say what each idea is and why it's important). Ask for feedback. Ask how people like the ideas and if they have any new ideas.
- Someone in your group records the feedback on a flip chart. You can write new ideas on 6"x8" cards and tape the cards to the map.

You will need:

- The map of the neighborhood you created in Activity 10
- A flip-chart or large sheets of newsprint paper
- Colored markers
- colored stickers for voting

- Have the people in the meeting vote on the ideas by putting stickers next to each idea. They should put a red sticker next to projects they think are "great," a yellow sticker for "OK" and a green sticker for "not OK." (They can do this right on the map.)
- Ask who would like to help you and how they think they could help you.

PLAN IT!

END PRODUCT: A list of ideas for projects with community support.

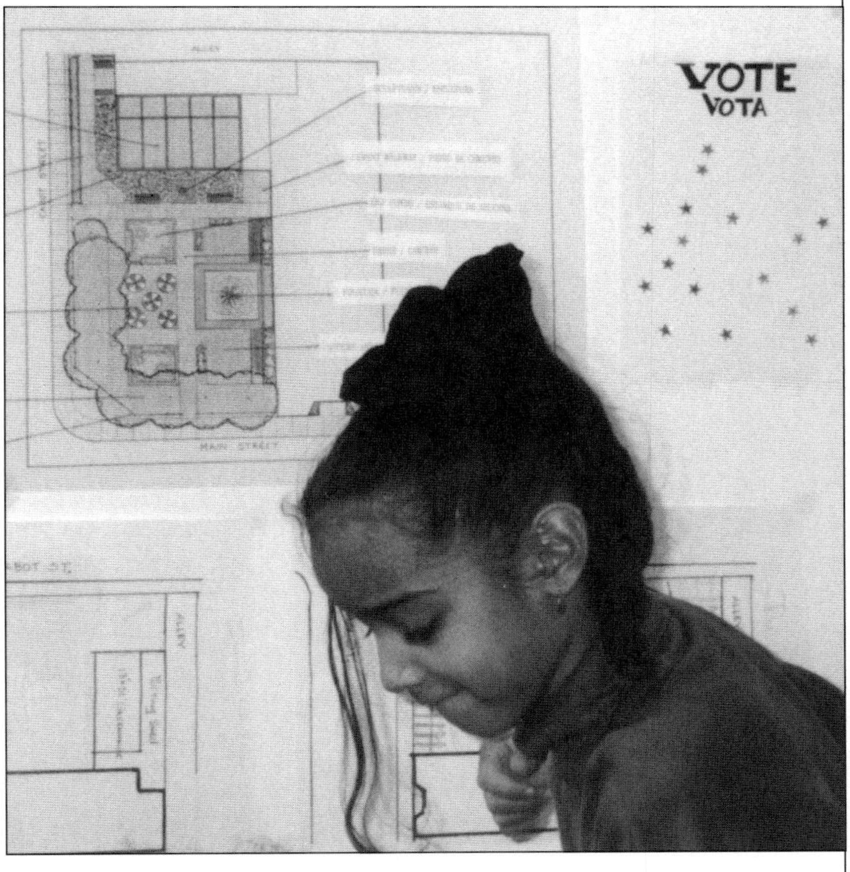

PLAN IT!

Let's do some projects!

WHAT TO DO FIRST

ACTIVITY **12**

PLAN IT!

12. Let's do some projects!

WHAT

Now it is time to decide which projects you are going to do **first**.

HOW

See Activity 9 Choosing the best ideas

See Activity 11 Getting community input

✷ **Review the list of the high priority projects** (worked out in the earlier activities, and from the feedback from the community and city officials).

- Write 5 to 10 of the best projects on the newsprint or flip-chart.

✷ **Look at each project and discuss when it can be done**. This is only a rough estimate at this stage.

- Next to each project write if it is:
  - ✔ Short-term (something you can do in one month)
  - ✔ Medium-term (something you could do in the next three to four months)
  - ✔ Long-term (something that will take more than four months either because it is complicated, or expensive, or because it has to come after other projects).

✷ **Decide on one or two projects you want to do first**. This might be really obvious or you may need to vote.

What you need:

- Large sheets of newsprint paper or a flip chart
- Large colored markers

END PRODUCT: One or two projects selected to work on first.

PLAN IT!

IDEAS FOR THE CANAL WALK

1. DRAW BRIDGE
2. CLEAN WATER
3. NEW BRIDGE
4. FOUNTAIN
5. SIDE WALK
6. FLOWERS
7. NEW FENCES
8. CLEAN EVERYTHING
9. MAKE A RESTAURANT
10. NO GANGS
11. FIX THE BUILDINGS
12. COLOR
13. WATER SLIDE
14. WATERFALL
15. DINER
16. NO BULLIES
17. RULES
18. PLAYGROUND
19. TUNNEL FOR PADDLE BOATS
20. POLICE MEN
21. A WALKWAY ACROSS THE WATER
22. BENCHES
23. MORE TREES
24. TRASH CANS
25. SMOOTH SURFACES
26. NO ALCOHOL
27. REST ROOMS
28. MURALS
29. HOUSES
30. PARKING LOT
31. NEW STREET
32. COBBLE STONE STREET
33. IN GROUND POOL
34. LIFE GUARDS
35. HORSE BACK RIDING
36. SWIMMING LESSONS
37. CUT DOWN RUSTY TREES
38. GREENHOUSE
39. CLUB HOUSES
40. FREE BOAT RIDES
41. ENTRANCE AND EXIT THAT IS BLOCKED AT NIGHT

PLAN IT!

PLAN IT!

Collaborating with other groups

ACTIVITY **13**

13. Collaborating with other groups

WHAT

Collaboration greatly expands the projects a group can be involved with. Three of such projects are described below. They involve collaborating with volunteer groups, an art gallery, and government. It is also possible to collaborate with other youth groups.

HOW

There are three basic models for collaboration:

- Partnership with other groups.
- Participation in an existing project or process where other people are in charge.
- Acting as consultants or experts.

These three models are described below through examples.

1. PARTNERSHIP: *Canal Walk and Centro Agricola*
Canal Walk

CANAL WALK MODEL WITH MAYOR

In the Canal Walk project, young people collaborated with Greater Holyoke, Inc., a community development corporation from the downtown; the Children's Museum located in the downtown; and the Canal Gallery, a local art gallery.

In this large project to design a walk along the nineteenth century canals that are along the edge of the South Holyoke neighborhood, YouthPower designed elements of the walk, such as sidewalk patterns and flags. These elements were incorporated into a model built by Americorps volunteers and located in the Canal Gallery. This project was far too large for a youth group alone but through collaboration young people were able to take part.

Centro Agricola

In this project, young people and community members worked together to design a plaza.

- Young people brainstormed some ideas for the plaza.
- These plans served as a basis for the three design concepts that were drawn by the project coordinators in a birds-eye view.
- Participants voted on the top three designs that were then presented by the young people to the public at an outdoor meeting in a tent.
- The community members then voted on the design they favored most by attaching stickers.

2. PARTICIPATION: Downtown Master Plan

YouthPower participated in workshop meetings looking at downtown redevelopment as part of the city-wide planning process. Their participation allowed a productive exchange of ideas to take place.

It allowed adults to gain a new perspective from young people and minorities as well as allowing the young people the opportunity to gain respect from adults and be heard as a voice in the community.

3. CONSULTATION: Master Plan

In another component of the master planning process, YouthPower also participated in the open space committee.

Turn the page...there's more!

Following a meeting where technical issues were discussed, the planning department sought to incorporate young people's ideas. The youth were asked to give a slide show and presentation to the Holyoke Planning Department showing the good and bad examples of open space, such as parks. In this case, the young people served as experts advising city officials on open space in their community.

This information will be used by the planning department to assist them in planning efforts for the city.

END PRODUCT: Projects completed that would not have been possible without collaboration.

Getting help and advice

ACTIVITY **14**

14. Getting help and advice

WHAT

People in a number of jobs and professions deal with issues of planning, design, and public art. Some of these people will live and work in your neighborhood, others are at City Hall. Many are happy to have you arrange to visit them or else to come speak to your group about your projects.

HOW and WHO

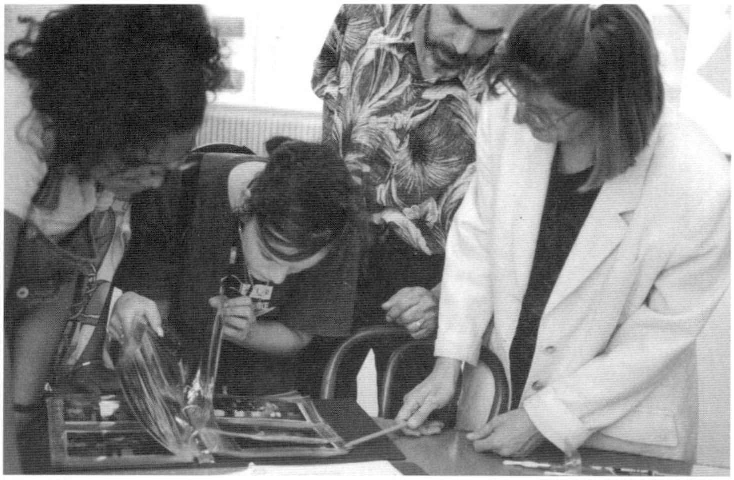

- **Architects** design and renovate buildings. You may know of architects with offices in your neighborhood. If buildings are being constructed or renovated by architects, there is often a sign in the front listing their names (along with the names of other professionals). The planning department in City Hall will also know of local architects. The American Institute of Architects chapter in your state can also help you contact architects. The national office can be contacted at http://www.aiaonline.com or by phoning 1 202 626 7300.
- **Landscape architects** design outdoor areas such as parks. You can find landscape architects in the same way you find architects. Their professional association is the American Society of Landscape Architects, 636 Eye Street, NW, Washington, DC 20001-3736, phone 202 898 2444, fax 202 898 1185, or http://www.asla.org/.
- **Planners** work at regulating and designing neighborhoods, cities, and regions. Most city and town governments have their own planners and they are

often available to talk with youth groups. The American Planning Association web page at http://www.planning.org has an informative section on K-12 education that is described in the "Further resources" section in part two of this manual. To contact the American Planning Association you can write to APA, 122 S. Michigan Avenue, Suite 1600, Chicago, IL 60603, or call 312-431-9100.

- **Builders and developers** do the work of developing and constructing buildings and some outdoor areas like playgrounds. You can find out about local builders and developers through the planning department in your town or city.
- The **government** of the city or town you live in probably employs people in a number of jobs including planning, engineering, park maintenance, and construction. The planning department and the community development office are the departments most likely to be interested in helping you. Your local city council member can often help you get in touch with the right people.
- Many neighborhoods have other groups that contain experts on your neighborhood such as people working for local **community development corporations**, members of the **Chamber of Commerce**, and volunteer officers of neighborhood associations or improvement societies.

END PRODUCT: Help in creating a better plan or project.

Making a timeline

FOR IMPROVING YOUR NEIGHBORHOOD

	Sept.	Oct.	Nov.	Dec.	Jan.	Feb.	Mar.	Apr.	May	June	July	Aug.
MAKE A MURAL												
● Find a place for the mural	X											
● Get permission to do it	X											
● Design the mural		X										
● Paint the mural		X										
● Celebrate			X									
REPAIR AND BEAUTIFY A PLAYGROUND												
● Visit the playground and see what needs to get fixed		X										
● Talk to Parks Department		X										
● Make a plan for fixing the playground			X									
● Get materials and volunteers				X	X	X						
● Fix the playground							X	X	X			
● Celebrate										X		
MAKE BANNERS FOR HISTORIC SITES												
● Research sites				X	X							
● Design banners						X	X					
● Get permission							X					
● Make the banners								X	X			
● Install the banners										X	X	
● Celebrate												X

ACTIVITY 15

15. Making a timeline for improving your neighborhood

See Basic Rules of Brainstorming in Activity 1.

What you need:

- Large sheets of newsprint
- Large colored markers

WHAT

Making a timeline lets you figure out what you need to do and when you need to do it.

HOW

✷ **For the projects that you have decided to do, brainstorm the steps that need to be done to complete each project** such as:

- Getting permission to work on the site.
- Designing the project.
- Getting materials for the project.
- Getting volunteers.
- Doing the project.

✷ **On the left side of the large sheet of paper, list each project with the steps needed to do it.**

✷ **Draw a line under each step across the entire sheet of paper.**

✷ **Then, across the top of the paper write a list of the 12 months**, starting with the current month, and draw a vertical line down between each month to the bottom of the page.

✷ **Look at each step and figure out which month it needs to happen in order to complete the project.** Try to make sure there are not too many things happening each month. If there are, shift some activity into the next month.

END PRODUCT: A work plan with both steps and a time line.

Some things you might think about when creating your timeline:

- **Do some activities need to be done at particular times of year like the summer or school holidays?**
- **Do some steps need to be done before others can be started?**

FOR A SAMPLE TIME LINE — TURN THE PAGE!

EXAMPLE TIMELINE FOR THREE PROJECTS

	Sept.	Oct.	Nov.	Dec.	Jan.	Feb.	Mar.	Apr.	May	June	July	Aug.
MAKE A MURAL												
● Find a place for the mural	X											
● Get permission to do it	X											
● Design the mural		X										
● Paint the mural		X										
● Celebrate			X									
REPAIR AND BEAUTIFY A PLAYGROUND												
● Visit the playground and list what needs to get fixed		X										
● Talk to Parks Department		X										
● Make a plan for fixing the playground			X									
● Get materials and volunteers				X	X	X						
● Fix the playground							X	X	X			
● Celebrate										X		
MAKE BANNERS FOR HISTORIC SITES												
● Research sites				X	X							
● Design banners						X	X					
● Get permission							X					
● Make the banners								X	X			
● Install the banners										X	X	
● Celebrate												X

Preparing to do a project

ACTIVITY 16

DO IT!

See Section Two: Vocabulary

16. Preparing to do a project

WHAT

This activity is about getting ready to do a project.

Many projects require that permits and permissions be obtained.

Construction often involves safety and liability issues.

HOW

Projects vary considerably in terms of the resources necessary and the steps for implementing them. The following checklist deals with issues that are important for most projects.

See Activity 14: Getting help and advice

See Activity 15: Making a timeline

✸ From the timeline created in Activity 15, you will have a list of steps to do the project. You can make a more detailed timeline for the project. See the example on the opposite page.

Check over the list of steps with someone who does this kind of project a lot. This could be a planner, architect, landscape architect, builder, and so on. Make sure you haven't missed anything important.

✸ **Find out if permissions and/or permits are needed and how to get them.** To do this:

- Communicate with the owner of the site to get their permission.
- Contact the city government, starting with the planning department, and ask them if anyone else needs to be contacted.
- Find out if you need to have insurance either to do the work, or for the long term management of the project. With your group leader, decide how to handle this.

✸ **Figure out the money and support that you need**, where you can get them, and who should do the work of getting the resources (e.g. young people or coordinators). Resources can be community support, money, and technical assistance.

- Community support can come from neighborhood associations, churches and temples, and other youth organizations.
- Money can come from grants, the city, local banks, and materials and equipment from local businesses. Ask some local experts how they raise money.
- Professional help can come from local professionals, colleges and universities, local service clubs, other youth groups, and parents.

END PRODUCT: *A group prepared to do a project.*

SAMPLE PROJECT TIMELINE

WHEN	WHO	WHAT	NOTES
April 15	all	measure the site	In this section, make notes about equipment you will need, activities the group will need to do for each step, things you need to check on, getting permission or approval, and people you need to contact.
April 17	peers and all	brainstorm ideas for playground	
April 20-30	1-2 peers	draw plans	
May 1-15	staff and peers	get Parks Dept approval	
May 15-20	staff and peers	make list of materials, equipment	
May 20-June 10	staff	plan project: make project work plan	
June 20-26	all	do the project	
June 30	staff, peers, and all	ceremony and publicity	

DO IT!

Drawing a plan for your project

ACTIVITY 17

DO IT!

17. Drawing a plan for your project

NOTE: This activity will require 2 or 3 sessions.

See Section 2: Design Basics for more details.

WHAT

This activity helps you draw a plan for your project.

HOW

✷ Visit the site and measure it.

- Make rough drawings showing the basic shape of the site.
- Teams of 2 to 4 people measure how big the site is and mark the measurements on the rough drawings. They should also show where any existing features are (such as equipment, buildings, and natural features like trees).

Things you will need:

- A long measuring tape
- Notepads for the site visits — to write down measurements and ideas for improvements
- Paper for drawing the plan
- Pens and pencils
- Architectural scale ruler
- Architect's triangle

✷ Visit the site and make a list of all the things you need to do to improve it. Bring the ideas you already have for the site and brainstorm new ones.

- The group should discuss the ideas and brainstorm new ones. Each team can have a notepad to write down the ideas.
- The teams should also mark on the rough drawings where they think the ideas should go.

✷ Decide which ideas work best.

- The group decides which plan is best or combines the best ideas into one plan.

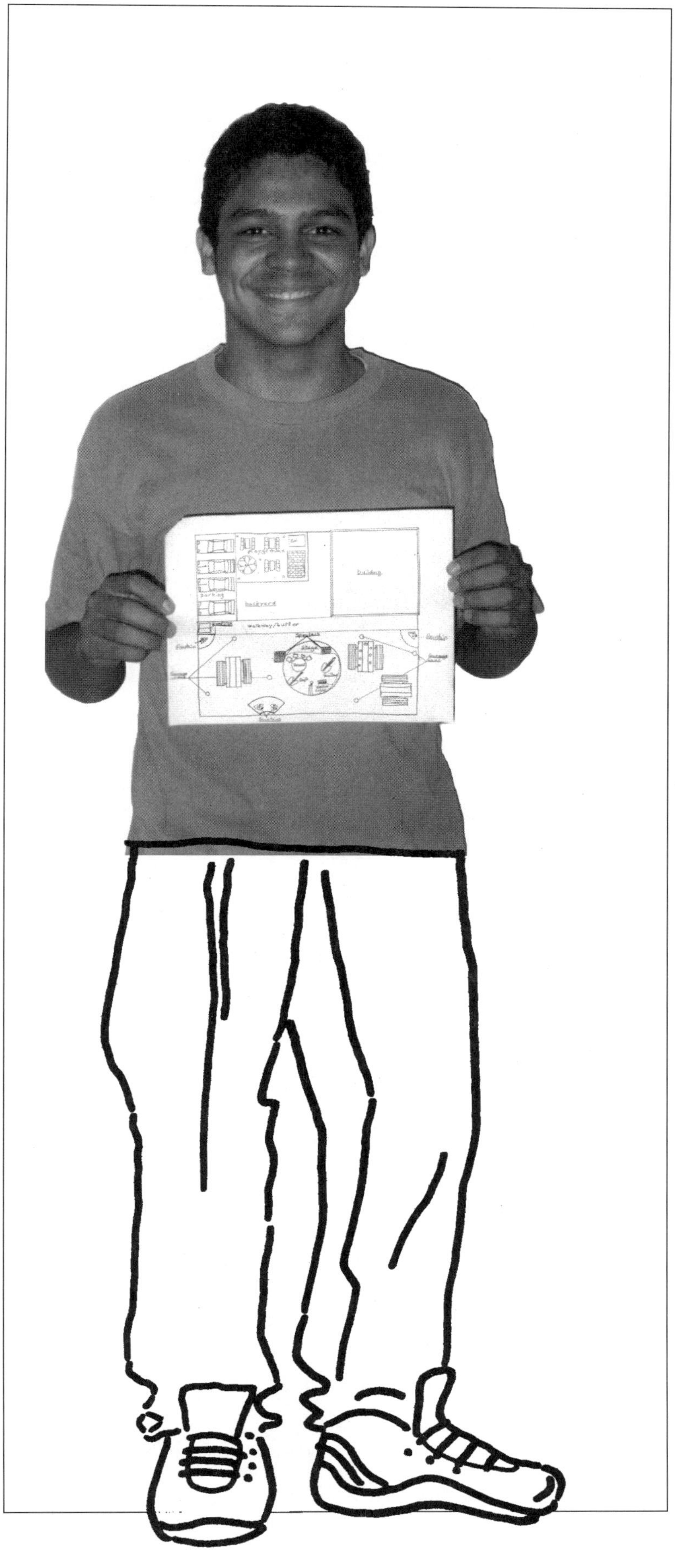

DO IT!

✸ **Draw your plan for the site.**

- One or 2 people are chosen to draw the plan for the site.
- The plan shows how big the site is, where things are, what is going to be removed or fixed, and where new things will go.

END PRODUCT: A drawn plan of the site with changes marked.

DO IT!

DO IT!

Making a project work plan

ACTIVITY 18

DO IT!

18. Making a project work plan

WHAT

The project work plan tells you all the tasks you need to do, who will do what task, when they will be done, and what materials you need. This is a much more specific and short-term plan than the one in Activity 15.

HOW

Things you will need:

- A flip chart or pad of newsprint paper
- Colored markers

✷ **Make a list of all the things you decided to do to improve the site.**

- Remember to include things you need to do to prepare for the project, and discuss the order in which things should happen.
- Write all the things on the flip chart, down the middle of the page.
- Discuss each task and what it involves. You can write notes next to each task.

✷ **Decide who will be the team leaders for each task** (and it is good to have 2 leaders for each task).

- Write the team leaders' names next to each task.

✷ **Decide when each task needs to be done** and write when next to each task. Make sure that you give enough time for each task.

✷ **Decide what materials and equipment are needed for each task** and write this on the right side of the paper.

- Go over the plan and make sure everyone understands what they will be doing.

END PRODUCT: Team leaders who know the tasks they are leading and the materials and equipment that they will need.

WORK PLAN EXAMPLE

WHEN	WHO	WHAT	NOTES & MATERIALS
Day before	Project staff, peer Leaders	Materials and equipment ready	See materials list, don't forget food
9:00-9:30	Staff,peers, all	On site meeting, form teams	Go over safety rules, tasks
9:30-11:30	Teams 1&2	Take apart broken benches	Wrenches, pry bar, screwdriver
9:30-11:30	Team 3	Clean up site	Rakes, brooms, shovels, garbage bags
9:30-11:30	Team 4	Put primer paint on playground equipment	Paint, paint buckets, brushes, gloves, water bucket
11:30-12:00	All	Lunch break	Pizza and soda
12:00-1:30	Team 1&2	Repair broken benches	Wood, saw, drill, screws, wrenches
12:00-1:30	Team 3	Paint playground equipment	Red, yellow, and blue paint, brushes, buckets, gloves
12:00-1:30	Team 4	Paint benches already primed	Yellow and blue paint, brushes, rollers, buckets, gloves
1:30-2:00	All	Clean up	Clean brushes, put equipment away, clean site

DO IT!

Doing the project

ACTIVITY 19

DO IT!

19. Doing the project

WHAT

This activity involves doing a project.

HOW

See Section 2: Instructions for coordinators

✷ **Check to make sure you have all the materials and equipment.**

✷ **Check that you have refreshments and a first aid kit.**

✷ **Have a meeting at the site before you start working.**

- Go over rules for the work, and especially safety rules. Demonstrate how to use tools and equipment.
- Explain the project work plan to the whole group.
- Divide the group into teams to work with the team leaders on specific tasks.
- A staff person and a peer are chosen to make sure safety rules are followed and that materials and equipment are taken care of.

✷ **Do the project.**

- Be sure to take breaks every two hours.
- Make sure all trash and extra materials are picked up and all equipment is cleaned and put away. (Make sure you give yourself enough time to do this.)

SKINNER BUILDING PAINT DAY

DO IT!

DO IT!

We completed our project--

NOW WHAT?

ACTIVITY 20

DO IT!

20. We completed our project, now what?

WHAT

Once a project is completed it needs to be maintained. Often there need to be rules for activities allowed in the space, and for who can use it. There also needs to be a way of maintaining it and keeping it clean.

HOW

✷ **Brainstorm the following:**

See Basic Rules of Brainstorming in Activity 1.

- The things about the project that you like.
- The things that could mess up the project.
- The existing rules and people that protect the project.

✷ If there could be a problem with using or maintaining the project, **discuss the most practical ideas for making sure the project doesn't get messed up**.

- You might like to answer the following questions:
    - Who is responsible for looking after the project? Is the city or a school responsible, for instance?
    - Can you make new rules?
    - Can you take responsibility for looking after it?
    - Is anyone else interested in the project, such as other youth groups and neighborhood organizations?

✷ **Make a plan for maintaining the project.** Meet with other people interested in the area, like people from the city government and neighbors, and show them your brainstorm ideas about keeping the project maintained. You can then jointly create a proposal for rules and a plan for maintenance.

- You may want to paint the rules on signs and post them, or you might assign specific maintenance tasks to different individuals.

END PRODUCT: A maintained project.

MAKING RULES

DO IT!

OTHER ACTIVITIES

Celebrations and awards

ACTIVITY 21

21. Celebrations and awards

See Activity 23: Getting publicity

WHAT

It is important to celebrate when projects are completed and give awards to participants and others who helped.

HOW

✸ **Plan an event to celebrate the success of your project. (It is best to have the event at the project site.)**

- Make invitations and send them to everyone who took part, supported, and is interested in the project.
- Write to newspapers, and local T.V. media and give a brief description of your project and the event you are planning. Call them up to encourage them to come.
- Decide if you are going to have food, refreshments, and music and what you are going to say.
- Prizes and awards can be given to individuals or teams in your group and others who helped or supported you.

YOU CAN GIVE AWARDS FOR:

- The neatest job.
- The most colorful.
- The team who cleaned up best.
- Individuals or groups who helped your group.
- Individuals or groups who participated.
- Individuals or groups who gave you financial support, like money, or donated materials and equipment.

IDEAS FOR AWARDS ARE:

- Certificates.
- Prizes.
- Plaques.
- Pictures.

END PRODUCT: Fun.

THANK YOU FOR HELPING

Recording the project

ACTIVITY 22

OTHER ACTIVITIES

22. Recording the project

WHAT

Recording a project helps you see what you achieved and is useful for persuading funding agencies to give further resources.

HOW

✷ **There are a lot of ways to document what you did. These include:**

- Notes from meetings and activities along with lists of those involved in each meeting.
- Drawings from the beginning stages and later stages.
- Photographs of people participating in the project — you can make picture boards of your activities and projects.
- "Official" drawings of the projects. These are often drawn by people like architects, landscape architects, builders, or engineers.
- Photos of the built work. "Before and after" photos are very helpful.
- Maps of the proposed projects with those completed marked clearly.
- Clippings from press coverage in the local paper.
- Letters of congratulation from residents or officials.

✷ **Put your records in a large 3 ring notebook and/or make posters or picture boards.**

END PRODUCT: A record of your achievements.

Getting publicity

ACTIVITY 23

23. Getting publicity

WHAT

It's important to provide publicity for the organization and for its successful projects. This publicity can be within the neighborhood and outside it.

- Neighborhood publicity, through presentations at neighborhood association meetings or articles in a neighborhood newsletter, allows participants to see and feel that their efforts are paying off and they are actually accomplishing things.
- Outside publicity, for example through the local newspaper, allows others outside the neighborhood to see what the young people in their community are achieving.

This promotes community pride, can help get others involved (recruiting), and may allow for possibilities of additional projects and collaborations.

HOW

✷ **Publicity doesn't just happen. You have to seek it out. The following activities will help you get publicity.**

- Call the local newspaper when you are going to have a construction or clean-up day and tell them to come for a photograph. It often helps to also send a press release, a short article on your project that lists (all on **one** page):
  - The title of the project.
  - The name and phone number of a contact person.
  - The organization doing the project.
  - A paragraph or two describing the project. This needs to be written as if it would go straight in a newspaper.
- Invite the mayor to a work day and call the paper to say that she or he will be there.

- When you know that a local festival or community fair is coming up, where organizations will be having displays, ask for a table and create a display of your own. With all the drawings and maps you will have produced you'll have lots of material for a display.
- Find out about local newsletters and write a short article for them or send in some photos. Lots of places have newsletters: neighborhood associations, community police districts, churches, temples, and sports clubs.

AWARD CEREMONY WITH PUBLICITY

END PRODUCT: Projects that people in your community know about.

OTHER ACTIVITIES

Young people speak out. . .

EVALUATING AND LEARNING FROM THE PROCESS

ACTIVITY 24

24. Young people speak out

WHAT

It is important to evaluate how things are going. This way you can learn from your successes and mistakes and make your project better. You can also do this throughout the year and not only when projects are ending. Once a month is a good amount.

See Basic Rules of Brainstorming in Activity 1.

HOW

✷ **Get everyone involved in the activity. Have them answer some of the following questions:**

- What was fun?
- What worked?
- What was frustrating?
- Did the group learn/accomplish something?
- How was group behavior?
- How did people work as a team?
- How was preparation (agenda, materials, etc.)?

✷ **Get people to explain reasons for their answers and brainstorm ideas for making things better.**

✷ **Use the list to help plan the next project.**

END PRODUCT: Improved work and more successful projects.

Example: YouthPower preparing this manual

One example of this was the process YouthPower went through in designing this manual. In one meeting we asked youth peer leaders two questions about the activities and projects they had participated in: What was fun and worked? What has been frustrating?

Fun things included:

- When we did things we actually planned to do.
- Going out with a video and recording ideas about the neighborhood.
- Hands-on activities.
- Being a peer leader.
- Pasting little pictures on maps to show where we wanted things to happen.

Frustrating things included:

- Having meetings without games or fun things.
- When there are too many people moving around in an activity.
- Not having enough time to prepare for meetings.

GROUP DOING EVALUATION

Section Two: More advice on doing these activities

About El Arco Iris and YouthPower

El Arco Iris is the youth arts program of Nueva Esperanza, Inc., a community development corporation located in South Holyoke, Massachusetts. In December 1995 El Arco Iris started the YouthPower Project to involve young people in planning and building a better neighborhood. The exercises in this book show some of the activities that have resulted.

The manual reflects the experiences of YouthPower and El Arco Iris working with young people living in the same small neighborhood. However, the exercises can be modified for groups drawing participants from a larger area, such as groups based at schools, temples, or churches. For example, instead of using the residential neighborhood as the focus for activities, these kinds of groups could explore the neighborhood where the group meets.

Design basics

I. Measuring the site

To draw the site for one of your projects, you need to know how big it is. Sometimes you can find maps or plans of the site that have already been drawn. But often you'll need to do it yourselves. These instructions can help you do that—at least well enough to develop some preliminary ideas and designs.

✷ **Quick method: Learn your own pace, then pace off the site.**

Any one person will walk with steps or paces that are about the same length—especially when walking at a similar speed. The following instructions can let you find the length of your own pace.

To do this exercise you'll need a tape measure that is fairly long—try to find one like the ones they use on construction sites. A tape measure that is one hundred feet long is best for this exercise. You'll also need to find a flat place that is easy to walk on and fairly large.

There are two ways to do this.

The first way is to find a comfortable walking speed that you can repeat and walk 10 paces and measure how far this is. Do it at least five times and average the number, and divide by 10 (for 10 paces) and that's the average length of a pace.

The other way to do this is to measure out 100 feet and then count the number of paces it takes to walk this (including parts of paces). Do this at least five times and average the number and then divide 100 feet by the number and that's the length your pace.

✷ **Measuring with a tape measure**

For more complicated sites or when you need to be more exact so you can actually build things, it helps to use a tape measure to measure the site. Using a 100-foot long tape measure is the easiest way to measure a site.

Be sure to measure by running your tape along the ground. Don't try to measure by holding it up in the air for long distances.

Measure from as many points as possible and from as many different directions as possible. That will help you make sure that your measurements are correct and accurate. It is better to take too many measurements than too few.

II. Evaluating existing conditions

A. Mapping activities

It is good to see what is already happening on site. Of course if it is a fenced-in vacant lot there may not be a lot happening, but where the area is currently being used the following activities can help you understand who uses it, how they use it, and when they use it.

Using a map of the site, find a place where you can observe the area without disturbing the activities that happen there. This can be quite difficult if you have to sit in the site and, for example, take up the only bench there.

But assuming you can find somewhere to sit or stand where you won't scare people away, go and observe the site at different times of the day and days of the week and map what is happening. Try to do this on both weekend days, and at least one week day, and in the morning, afternoon, and evening.

A good way to do this is to copy enough maps so you can draw on a new one every 15 minutes, then every 15 minutes you should note down on the map who is in the area, what they are doing, and where they are doing it. You can then combine the maps using different colors for different kinds of people or types of activities or times of day. Be sure to label each map with the time of day and the day of the week, and other information that might affect activities, such as the weather.

III. Beginning to design

A. Understanding design as a process

It is important when you design, not to fall in love with your first idea. It may seem great to you, but good designs come from a process that requires lots of revisions of your first ideas.

Try to think about all the possible problems with a design. Don't ignore problems just because you love your design! Think about how different people will use the place. Get the opinions of other people — friends, neighbors, professionals, and other people who might use the place. Use their opinions to improve your original idea. Be open to suggestions — revisions are part of making a good idea better.

AXIS

B. Basic design principles

It may be helpful to you to understand some basic elements of design. There are a lot of design principles, but some of the major ones are: axis, symmetry, asymmetry, hierarchy, rhythm and repetition (see F. Ching's *Architecture: Form, Space, and Order*, 1979, Van Nostrand Reinhold).

Once you become familiar with these design principles, you will start to see that they are used in many places throughout your neighborhood. They don't necessarily make a place or a design "good," but they do help to make the space feel more organized.

AXIS

AXIS:
An axis is a straight line that connects two objects or places.

For instance, if a fountain or a statue lines up with the entrance to a building, the are said to be "on axis" with each other.

The line or axis that connects two things can be imaginary or "implied" indirectly, meaning that there is no line on the ground telling you that these two things are connected. At other times this line can be made obvious by making it visible, through such things as paving patterns or rows or trees that reinforce or "define" its edges.

SYMMETRY:
Symmetry means that one side is the exact mirror image of the other side. For instance, the human body has symmetry or "is symmetrical." If a line can be easily drawn down the middle of a design, and one

SYMMETRY

SYMMETRY

side is like a mirror reflection of the other wide, then that design is said to be symmetrical.

ASYMMETRY

ASYMMETRY:

Asymmetry is the lack of symmetry. In other words, if one side does not look exactly like the other side it is "asymmetrical." This does not mean that the design is not carefully arranged according to some design principles -- it is just not symmetrical.

ASYMMETRY

HIERARCHY:

Hierarchy means that something is more important than other things. Usually in hierarchy there is a clear rank order from most important to least important.

HIERARCHY

In landscape design and architecture this means that one space is more important than the others. Usually you know this because it is obviously different — larger, sunnier, or is located in some important area. The colors used in this important area might be different than colors used throughout the rest of the design. Or the rest of the design might be done in rectangles while the important space is a circle. The difference must be obvious in order to make it obvious to people that there is a hierarchy.

HIERARCHY

If you want to make a space that is more important than the other spaces, then you need to give it an important location, or size, or color, or even shape.

REPETITION

REPETITION:

Repetition means that something is repeated over and over again. This can be very important in a design. If you do not repeat anything, and if each and every element of a design is different, than the design might feel chaotic, messy, and confusing to people who use the space.

REPETITION

What you decide to repeat in a design is really up to you. You can repeat shapes (squares, circles) or materials (brick paving or a particular type of tree) or color.

RHYTHM:

RHYTHM

When you repeat an element in a certain regular order or pattern, then you have set up a rhythm. Rhythm can be seen in the posts of a fence, or in a row of identical houses, or a row of trees that are spaced the same distance apart.

You can set up rhythm in your design by alternating trees with low planter boxes, or brick paving with concrete paving.

RHYTHM

FORMAL vs. INFORMAL

FORMAL

Often landscape designs are referred to as "formal" or "informal." Formal designs are often designs that are symmetrical, that have a central axis, and that have lots of strong geometric forms. Informal designs are usually asymmetrical and are thought to look more "natural" because they use more curved lines and forms.

These are very general terms. Your design may end up having areas that are formal, and other areas that are informal in their design.

INFORMAL

SCALE:

The word scale has a lot of different meanings. In design, it often means a way of judging size or proportions relative to something else — like your own body, or the number of people that will be using the space, or as it relates to the building it is next to, or as it relates to the larger landscape. These "scale" measurements are hard to measure exactly and depend on the particular situation.

However, one of the most important "scales" by which to judge a space is the human body. Does the space feel too small for you? Or is it so large that you feel unprotected and exposed? If you know the story of "Goldilocks and the Three Bears," think about how Goldilocks had to sit in three different chairs until she found one that was just right.

If the space feels good — if the proportions seem right for the people who will use it — then it is said to have a "human scale" or a "good sense of scale."

C. Environmental impact of design

The ways in which you physically change the world around you might have an impact on other parts of the environment. Some things to keep in mind as you design:

✷ Are the materials that you are working with toxic? Some paints, for instance, might be more environmentally friendly than others. Check with your hardware store or the people you get your supplies from. They should be able to recommend the products that are least harmful to the environment.

✷ How should you remove existing materials from the site? Check with your city officials or other professionals to see if there are any materials—like lead paint or asbestos—on your site that need to have special procedures for removal them or disposal.

✷ How do you get rid of stuff on the site? Be sure that everything you remove gets disposed of properly. If you are digging, you might find old tires or old building rubble buried in your site. You may need to get a permit take these to the nearest landfill.

✷ There may be toxic substances such as lead in the soil. Be sure to have the soil tested before you begin working in it. Often local councils or universities can find people to do this for a low fee or even for free.

✷ In general, plants are more beneficial to the environment than paved surfaces such as asphalt or concrete. Plants produce oxygen for us to breathe and they cool the air. They also help to clean the water as rain falls and runs off into storm water sewers. Whenever possible include plants in your design.

✷ Try to select plants that require very little water. If plants are said to be "drought tolerant" then they can usually live without being watered every day. These types of plants are best, since using lots of water has negative effects on the larger environment.

D. Barrier-free design

Many people who use your design will be older people who cannot walk as well as young people. People in wheelchairs should also be able to use your site. For these people you want to remember to include the following in your design:

✸ Areas that can be entered without going up or down steps. These areas could be at ground level, or they could be entered by a ramp that slopes up or down into the space.

✸ Ramps should be long with a very gradual slope. The recommended slope is one inch going up or down for every twelve inches long.

E. Crime Prevention Through Design

Many people worry that crimes will take place in public spaces. There are things that you can do in the design of your site that will reduce the possibilities of crimes taking place and make the users feel more safe.

✸ Allow people to see into, out of, and around the area. Plants, especially bushes, should be low enough for you to see over them and to see any people behind them. Trees can be used if they have a high "canopy" and they don't have low branches, so people can see under and around the trees. You should be able to see through fences. Lighting should illuminate the entire space at night. People should be able to see into the space from the street and surrounding buildings without their view being blocked by plants, fences, benches, or buildings.

✸ Have the area locked up at night. Putting up a fence that can be controlled and locked during certain hours may keep out unwelcome people and activities.

✷ Have clear entrances and paths through the space. The people who use the site should be able to see a safe way out at all times. There must be more than one entrance, and the path leading to it should not be hidden by plants, benches, or fences.

IV. Visualizing your design

A. Types of drawings

✷ **sketches**

Sketches are like drawn photographs—they show what a place or thing looks like. However, they are not quite like photographs because you can choose to include some things and not others.

Although some people have a natural talent for sketching, it is also a skill that can be learned. There are many techniques for learning to sketch and it may be useful to have a local art teacher or artist come and show you some of these skills.

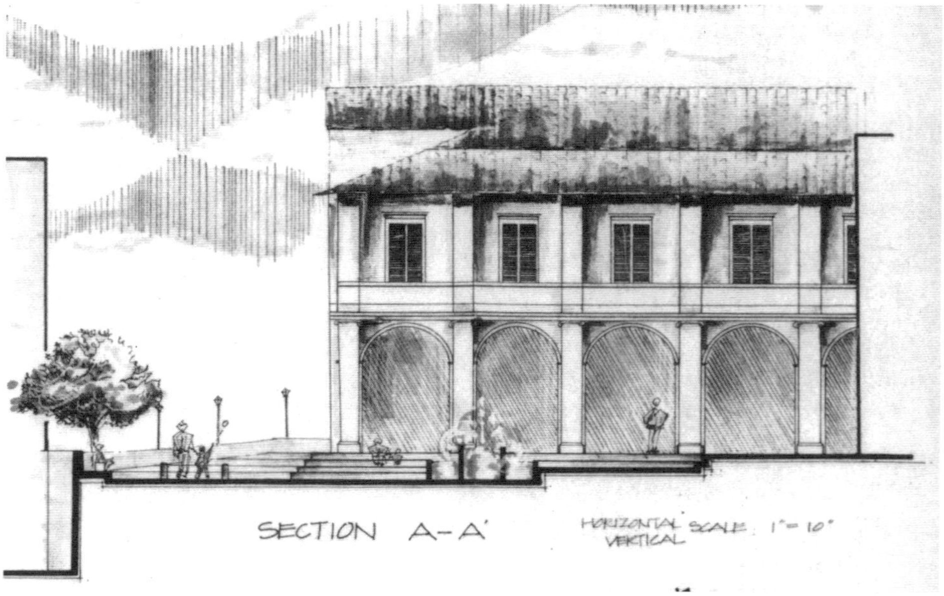

✷ plans, sections, elevations

A plan is the view looking down on something. Sometimes it is drawn like a picture taken from an airplane but often it is drawn as a horizontal slice through a building or site, as if everything about eye height was sliced off. The picture below is the plan of a complicated plaza.

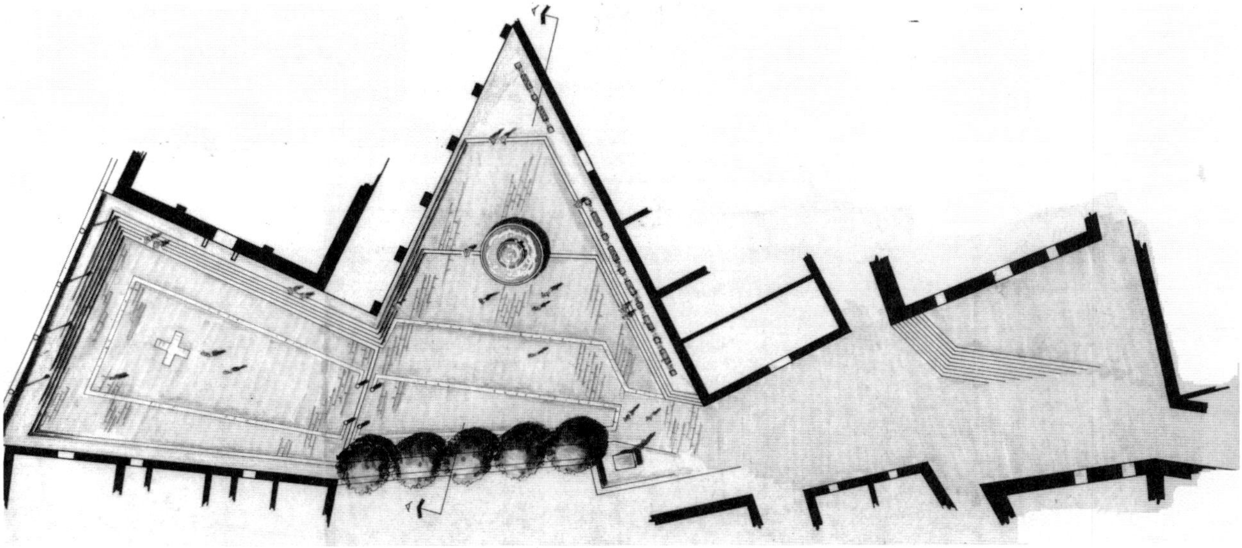

A section is a drawing of a site or building sliced vertically. It is as if someone took a knife and cut through the building or area from top to bottom. This shows the heights of things.

An elevation is a kind of picture of the exterior of a building. The illustration combines a section (the cut through the plaza) and an elevation (the view of the building behind).

If you would like more information on these different types of drawings, some good books are:
Architectural Graphics, Francis Ching, 1996, VNR.
Plan Graphics, T. Walker & D. Davis, 1990, VNR.
Landscape Graphics, Grant Reid, 1987, Whitney.
Drawing the Landscape, Chip Sullivan, 1997, VNR.

B. Making models

If you are going to be showing your design to other people, a model is usually the best way to do it, since they may not be able to understand plans and other drawings.

Helpful things to have for building a model include:
• a plan drawing of your proposed design.
• elevation drawings of buildings and other structures.
• sheets of cardboard (corrugated cardboard, thick "chip board," or foam core board.
• glue (white "Elmer's glue," or a hot glue gun, or carpenter's glue).
• utility knife and extra blades.
• "x-acto" knife and extra blades.
• metal ruler or straight edge.
• a variety of materials that you could use to show different surfaces, such as fabric, sand paper, colored construction paper, toothpicks, cotton balls, crayons, colored markers, clay, paint, twigs, aquarium gravel, etc.

Don't forget to include scale people in your model. You can make people out of clay or cardboard. They will give everyone looking at the model an idea of how big the spaces are and how tall the trees and buildings are.

For more information about building models, a good book is:
Why Design? by Anna Slafer & Kevin Cahill, Chicago Review Press, 1995.

Instructions for Coordinators

INTRODUCTION

These guidelines are primarily for the adult coordinators/supervisors of the project. They are basic guidelines and adults with experience working with youth may find some of the suggestions simplistic or obvious. It is also impossible to address all the situations that can arise; you are encouraged to use your own experience, intuition and creativity. Also keep in mind that the fundamental principle of YouthPower is that youth are empowered to make choices, take responsibility, and take an active role in planning and implementing.

PART I. SOME BASIC PRINCIPLES

SINCERITY AND RESPECT ARE KEY. It is important to convey to young people that you respect their ideas and opinions and that you take them seriously. Let them know that you hear their ideas by responding to them and acting upon them. Many youth feel that adults do not really care about or bother to listen to their opinions and they are extremely sensitive to criticism. This doesn't mean you have to always agree. If you disagree, honor their point of view and explain why you disagree. This does not mean that you cannot set high standards — in fact young people like challenges.

ENABLE THE YOUTH TO TAKE OWNERSHIP AND LEADERSHIP. This is the most fundamental principle of YouthPower. Your basic role will be to give the youth the guidance and tools they need to make informed decisions and to work effectively as a team. This is more of an art than a science. The difference between having ultimate responsibility and authority as an adult and empowering youth to be leaders is difficult to define. You will need to balance giving direction and maintaining order with allowing the youth to define their own direction and to create and abide by their own rules. The difference between guidance and taking over changes with different situations and the experience of the group.

The most difficult stage is the initial stage when the youth are uncertain about their role, not sure how to take on a leadership role, and still have the expectation that the adult is in full control. Especially in the beginning, they often will be shy about taking an active role. You will need to avoid the temptation to fill the void. Remember, once a pattern is set it is very difficult to undo. It's better to let the participants make a few mistakes than to be always correcting them.

TEAMWORK IS ESSENTIAL. Being part of a group is important to young people. Building a team that can work together and get along is critical to the success of the project. It is also very effective to break the larger group into smaller teams to work together on tasks. The smaller teams can share what they accomplished with the larger group. Smaller teams can also compete in games.

ASK QUESTIONS - AND LISTEN TO THE ANSWERS. DON'T LECTURE. Ask the right questions so the youth come up with answers. This in itself can be a challenge. Often — especially early in the process — questions or attempts to engage the group are met with little or no response. You will have to experiment with ways to bring people out. For example, you can start by asking people to raise their hands if they agree with a statement and then ask individuals to explain why. The trick is to think of the questions that will lead them to come up with the answers. Avoid lecturing (at almost all costs)! Of course there will be times when you will need to explain things. Be direct and concrete. Avoid academic or technical language that might make them feel confused or ignorant. This doesn't mean talking down to young people (that's worse than talking over their heads).

KEEP IT FUN. If it's not fun, they won't come. The most common complaint is "It's boring." Think of fun ways to run the meetings. For example, games can be used for people to say their ideas and have the others try to guess. Have at least one game or "energizer" during each meeting. Also youth are always more interested in participating in activities that are led by other youth, so having youth leaders is key.

PART II. OVERVIEW OF THE PLANNING AND DESIGN PROCESS AND USING THE GUIDE

1. THE PLANNING AND DESIGN PROCESS. There are some basic and necessary steps to the planning and design process. These steps are all included in the Guide, but it may be helpful to outline them here to give you an overview.

- Define your purpose and goals
- Identify the problems and opportunities of the area you are working with
- Brainstorm ideas
- Evaluate and prioritize the ideas
- Choose some ideas
- Implement them
- Reflect on how it all went

2. USING THE GUIDE. The Guide is organized to take you through a step-by-step process of developing a plan for improving your community and then planning, designing and implementing specific projects that will help to realize that plan. The Guide can also be used for smaller scale and shorter term endeavors. One of the first choices you will need to make is deciding on the scope of your project. Do you want to focus on a specific well-defined project or are you going to attempt to create a long-range plan for your community or neighborhood and work on a number of projects over time? Or you may be interested in particular kinds of projects such as green space or clean up or beautification.

The Guide uses a "neighborhood" or "community" as an example, but the principles and steps can also be applied to a town, park, green space or any other area your group is working on. You should use and adapt the Guide to serve your particular project. You are encouraged to be creative. The Guide is meant to guide you, not dictate what to do. You may find that not all chapters are relevant to your project or you may want to modify some of the exercises to meet your needs. Nevertheless, we feel any successful project must include the basic elements described in the guide: Build your team, dream it, plan it, and do it.

Good luck . . . . and have fun!!

PART III. GUIDELINES FOR CHAPTERS IN THE GUIDE

1. BUILDING A CORE GROUP AND DECIDING ON YOUR PURPOSE:

The first step: find a core group of youth who will "buy into the project."

- Your very first step as a project "coordinator" is to find and build a core group of young people who will "buy into" the project and take "ownership" of it. You may already have a group of youth that you work with or you may need to do outreach to create a new group.

- Starting small with a core group of three to five youth has the advantage of having those youth help to recruit and engage other young people. It is always more effective to have youth working with youth.

Engage the youth at the start in defining the goals and purpose.

- Whether you are starting with an existing group or creating a new one, you will have the challenge of getting the youth to understand, in general, what the project is about without making them feel like you are telling them what it is about. If you come across as the person who is deciding what to do and what is important, they will tend to take a passive role and become uninterested. On the other hand, if you are too vague, they may become confused and lose focus. Young people respond better to concrete examples than abstract concepts.

- You may want to have a brainstorming session for the core group similar to the one described in chapter four. This will help them get some of their ideas out. You should be careful not to have them develop ideas that are too definite, however, or the new people will not have the chance to give their ideas and feel part of the process.

2. WORKING AS A TEAM.

Building a team is a long term process and requires commitment.

✷ Teams are not built overnight. It takes time for people to become comfortable, find their place in the team and learn how to work together. Let the youth know that it will take time and requires commitment.

✷ Having the youth develop a contract for team members is a good way for them to set some ground rules and goals and show commitment. It also helps them take ownership for their team.

✷ Discuss with the youth what your and their expectations are and have them develop a set of rules to guide the daily meetings. It is good to review these at the beginning of each meeting.

Be aware of group dynamics.

✷ Group dynamics and the social aspects of working as a team are at least as important as the mechanics of planning and implementing the project. You should be prepared to deal with issues of control and leadership, romance and jealousy, cliques and exclusion.

✷ It is beyond the scope of this guide to give specific ways to deal with these situations, but it is a good idea to address them up front and have some guidelines in the rules.

Develop routines.

✷ Having routines helps develop familiarity, predictability and cohesiveness. They help the team members feel comfortable and help them to find their place in the team. Having consistency and routines also allows the youth to get good at doing things and to develop confidence. It also helps the youth feel secure that there is something they can depend on. A standard meeting agenda is a good way to do this (see below).

✷ Also be aware that routines can get boring and sometimes it is good to break the routines and do something completely different.

Train the group in the mechanics of working as a team.

✷ Explain how to develop an agenda and take minutes. Agendas should include a review of the minutes of the last meeting if applicable, a review of the agenda items, one or more main agenda items, a time and place for the next meeting, and a time at the end to reflect and/or evaluate. It is also good to start with a review of the ground rules, and to have an energizer in the middle.

✷ The team should also know how to develop an action plan for planning and implementing projects. The action plan should include who is responsible for each activity, when it must be completed by, and a clear description of the activity with enough information to be able to do it.

Train and practice the essential skills.

* The youth need to be trained in the basic skills for planning, decision making, and presenting.
* For planning they need to know how to brainstorm, evaluate, and make a work plan.

* For decision making they need to know how to decide by majority or by consensus.

* For presenting they need to know how to plan a meeting, assign roles, speak clearly and loudly enough, and how to engage the audience.

Decide how you are going to make decisions.

* The youth should be part of the decision making process and it is important to set up clear and consistent decision making processes. Voting/majority rules is a simple way of making decisions and works in many cases. In a small group, consensus sometimes works better for important decisions to maintain group cohesion.

* The adult coordinator should also make it clear that there may be certain decisions that s/he may need to make, such as making sure the project fits funder requirements or town/city regulations.

Everyone should have a role and responsibilities.

* Make sure that all the team members are given roles such as taking notes of meetings, leading meetings, writing on the flip chart, keeping track of time, etc. It works well to have youth work in pairs also.

Take time to reflect, evaluate, discuss problems, and come up with solutions.

* It is important to have a regular time to reflect on learning, evaluate the project, discuss problems, and come up with solutions. A form can be very helpful in this process. The form should fit your program, be easy to use and fun. The form allows each participant to put down his or her own thoughts and then share and discuss them as a group. It is important to act as quickly as possible to implement any suggestions.

3. OUTREACH

Decide on how you are going to explain your project.

* Once you know what your purpose is and you have a general idea of what you are going to do, you need to decide how you are going to explain it to other youth that you want to recruit for your project.

* Look to your core group to come up with both verbal and graphic ways to describe the project and work with them to design a flyer and informational material.

* Do not try to say too much. Think of key things that would make youth want to be part of your project. The core group will have a much better idea of how to reach their peers than an adult does.

Brainstorm ways to reach people.

* You can recruit internally in your organization, have the core group outreach to family and friends, do door-to-door outreach, make presentations to other youth groups, or distribute informational materials to other programs and/or people in the neighborhood.

* Face-to-face outreach is more effective than trying to recruit by sending written materials.

* It is important to have the youth actively involved in doing the outreach.

Develop an outreach and recruitment plan.

* Decide on one or more ways to do outreach. Decide how many people you want to recruit and how many people you think you should outreach to. Decide when you are going to do the outreach, who is going to do it and how you are going to do it.

* Have a sign-up sheet or membership form to have people sign or to give to them. Make sure the instructions are clear and there is contact information (name and phone number).

* The group should practice with each other before going out so they feel confident. Also before doing any door-to-door outreach, make sure everyone in the group knows the basic safety guidelines: always work at least in pairs; always have an adult back up; know how to avoid and/or handle belligerent people or dangerous situations (never be confrontational and leave as quickly as possible).

Selection and orientation.

* Decide how you are going to select members of the team (if more sign up than you can handle). Is it going to be first-come first-served, or are you going to interview and select people based on criteria such as interest and commitment? Work with the youth to design an orientation session for new members.

* The orientation should cover the project's purpose and goals, the basic ground rules, and the contract. It should also be fun and give the new participants the opportunity to express their ideas and feelings.

4. BRAINSTORMING A VISION OF YOUR IDEAL COMMUNITY

Brainstorming a vision is the key to engaging young people.

* This is the one process that early on will engage all the participants and give them a sense of ownership. It will also help to create the inspiration that will sustain the project over time. Without a vision and a dream, there will be no excitement or energy.

Brainstorming should be fun and creative.

* The purpose of this activity is not necessarily to come up with realistic or doable ideas but to give the participants the opportunity to express their ideas, their dreams, and their visions. It should be a fun and creative process. There is no right way to do this activity. It's okay to use any combination of pictures, symbols, words, etc. Let the group work out how they want to do it.

Everyone should be included.

* You may need to go around to the different groups and make sure that everyone is included.

* Encourage people who are shy or have low self-esteem to give their ideas.

Avoid evaluating ideas.

* This is not the time to dampen the creativity and spontaneity by saying an idea is too unrealistic or expensive or complicated or weird.

Look for the essence of the ideas.

* Some of the craziest ideas have good points. For example, someone might suggest building a water park or amusement park. This may not be feasible because of space and cost, but the idea of having a place with water where you can play is a good one. It may be feasible to get the city to install a sprinkler pool and playground equipment.

* Have the group discuss the ideas and say why they chose them and why they are important to them.

5. HOW DO YOU EXPERIENCE YOUR COMMUNITY?

Understanding how the group sees their community is important.

* This activity can reveal very important things about how people in the group experience their community.

There are many ways to do this.

⁕ The guide gives one example. In addition to where people do and don't go, you may want to discuss things like safety, drugs, and visual, olfactory and noise pollution.

6. THE NEIGHBORHOOD TOUR

Working in teams works best.

⁕ It works best to have the group work in teams of two to four. Have each team pick someone to write down the ideas and one or two people to present them.

Have each team present their ideas.

⁕ When the teams are done, they should present their ideas to the rest of the group. This is an excellent way to share a lot of ideas and gives the teams experience in presenting.

Make sure to keep good records.

⁕ The information you gather from the neighborhood tour is very valuable. Make sure you have copies of the teams' ideas and any other records such as photos and video and keep them in a file or safe place.

⁕ Another way of keeping records that is more fun and can engage the youth is to make a scrapbook and/or poster boards of different stages of the project.

7. MAKING A MAP OF WHAT'S GOOD AND WHAT'S BAD

Be creative with your map.

⁕ The Guide gives a suggestion for making a "community map." You can add drawn pictures, quotes, and could also use video footage to make a short video to go with the drawn map.

8. COMING UP WITH IDEAS TO IMPROVE THE COMMUNITY

This is different than brainstorming a vision for the community.

⁕ This activity requires coming up with specific ideas for specific needs.

⁕ Although you can still use brainstorming to come up with ideas, they should be more or less realistic and relevant to the neighborhood/community/project.

Be sure to use the ideas and information you have already gathered.

- Use the ideas from the vision map to help come up with more concrete ideas for the particular project.

- Use the information from the neighborhood tour to get more ideas of what is needed.

- Have the vision map and the map of what's good and bad displayed for everyone to see.

Some other ways to do this activity.

- Getting people to think outside of the box of their own particular perspective can be challenging. One way to get around this is by role playing. You can have teams of two to four role play different types of people such as the elderly, toddlers, families, youth, different ethnic groups, business people, etc. Each team then can come up with ideas of what kind of place they would like and present to the rest of the group.

- The participants can work in teams to review the vision map and the what's good and bad map and then compete to see which team can come up with the most ideas.

9. CHOOSING THE BEST IDEAS

This step is one of the most important steps. This is when you evaluate the ideas and decide which ones to include in your plan. It is important that your evaluation addresses both the needs of your group and the needs of the community.

- In the Guide, fun, learning potential, and community service are given as examples.

- Your group will need to decide what are their most important criteria for choosing the ideas. Your group should have a discussion about what factors they choose to evaluate the ideas and why.

- You can also use this process to make sure that ideas answer the needs of different people in the community such as the elderly, families, ethnic groups, and different aged youth.

- You can also use this process to make sure the ideas address important functions such as socializing, play, business activity, and culture.

Other variations of this process.

- As indicated above, this process can be relatively simple or quite complex.

- You can have the participants mark their three most important ideas and see which ones get the most votes.

✷ You can have teams work together to chose the ideas they like best. Then each team can present their ideas. You can choose the ideas that each team agrees on or have the whole group vote on the ideas they like best after the discussion.

✷ You can use a numbering system to score the ideas. For example "great" can equal 2, "OK" = 1, and "not OK" = 0. For each idea you can add the number of "great," "OK," and "not OK" answers and score each idea.
✷ If you are using several criteria to evaluate the ideas, you may need to "weight" the criteria. For example, you may decide that community service is twice as important as learning.

✷ An alternative is to choose "threshold" criteria. For example you may decide that fun is a threshold criteria. Even if an idea scores high in other areas, if it doesn't score high on fun it would not be included in the final selection.

✷ It is a good idea to have a discussion at the end for each person to say why he or she liked the ideas they chose.

10. MAKING A MAP OF THE IDEAS TO MAKE YOUR COMMUNITY BETTER

Another way to show your ideas on a map is with "icons."

✷ Icons are small simple pictures or symbols that represent your ideas. For example, a picture of a swing could represent a playground and a picture of a basketball hoop could represent a basketball court. (You will need to show what each icon means somewhere on the map.)

✷ Since icons can be smaller than pictures, it is easier to show more ideas in a smaller space with icons that with drawn pictures.

✷ You can often place the icons right on the sites on your map, which makes it easier to read than having to follow a line to the site.

The community map is an important visual representation of your group's ideas.

✷ It can be used to inform others in the community of your ideas and get their input.

✷ Maps and pictures are truly worth a thousand words. People will respond much better and have a better understanding of your ideas from a map and pictures.

You can use community maps to show existing conditions, your ideas, and projects completed. (See also Making a Map of What's Good and Bad in Your Community.)

* You can make a map with pictures of your community, showing the good and bad things and sites that need to be improved, another map of your ideas, and a third map with pictures of projects you complete.

11. GETTING COMMUNITY INPUT AND SUPPORT

It is important to know how others in your community respond to your ideas.

* Make sure you give people a chance to say if they don't like certain ideas and why. For example, residents of an apartment building may not want a basketball court next to their apartments because people playing at night would make noise.

* Make sure you identify groups that are excited about your ideas and would like to help. (See the chapter on collaborating.)

Make sure you get input and support from key "players" (groups that have influence or decision making powers in your community) and "stakeholders" (people and groups who will be affected by your project).

* Some key players are the City Council, the Planning Board, the Public Works Department and some stakeholders are residents of the community, business people, and property owners.

* You can have a discussion with your group about who the key players and stakeholders are and why they are important.

It is a big challenge to get people to come to meetings. You will need to do intensive outreach or try other ways to get people's input.

* Direct outreach works best but takes a lot of time and effort.

* If you send invitations by mail, make sure they give all the important information (what, why, where, when, who and how to contact).

* Follow up invitations with a reminder card and/or phone call, if possible. Ask for a commitment to come and bring other people.

* Other ways to get input are by approaching people directly with surveys/questionnaires or by having small "focus groups" where you work with small groups on specific questions.

Make sure you record the input and ideas.

* You can keep minutes or records of the meeting.

* You can use surveys or questionnaires.

12. LET'S DO SOME PROJECTS

This is a time for your group to decide which projects they can do. Some things to consider are:

- Does your group have the capacity (enough people, technical skills, etc.) to do the project?
- Do you have the money or resources to do the project?
- Do you have permission from the owner of the property and/or the city/town to do the project?

Don't immediately eliminate a project if it fails to meet any of the questions above.

- Brainstorm ways you could make the project work. For example if you don't have the money or resources to do the project, brainstorm how you might be able to work with the city to get funds and/or collaborate with other groups (see below).

13. COLLABORATING WITH OTHER GROUPS

There are many good reasons to collaborate with other groups:

- More people can help you get the project done faster and better. (Remember though that more isn't always better.)
- Other groups and organizations can offer resources and technical skills you might not have.
- Collaborating can help you get the community, political, and financial support you need to do the project.
- Collaborating is often necessary in order to do larger and more complex projects.

Collaborating is also complex and time consuming. Be aware of the "costs" of collaborating.

- Collaborating requires attending planning and evaluation meetings with other groups and keeping in close communication with them.
- Collaborating requires making decisions with other groups. This can slow things down and may mean that you will need to compromise.
- It is important to be very clear from the start who is going to do what and who has what powers.

14. GETTING HELP AND ADVICE

Know when you need help and advice.

- Professionals can help you avoid errors and help you to solve problems that would be difficult or impossible for you to solve.

Make sure the people helping you understand your needs and the needs of your community.

- Professionals can have a limited and rigid idea of how things should be done. They also do not necessarily understand the needs of your community.

15. MAKING A TIMELINE TO IMPROVE YOUR COMMUNITY

Especially at the beginning, it is very important to try to not do too many projects. It's better to do fewer projects well than it is to not succeed at a lot of projects.

- You should consider how realistic your timeline is.

- Prioritize the most important projects on your timeline, so you are prepared to drop some if necessary.

Also make sure to keep in mind the seasons and how they will affect certain stages of the project.

- Try to plan your project so that the planning activities are in bad weather times and the outside building activities are in good weather.

16. PREPARING TO DO A PROJECT

Get your group involved in brainstorming and figuring out the necessary steps of the project.

- The more involvement the group has in planning the project, the more ownership they will feel.

- This process also mentally prepares them for all the steps and the time it may take to get to the point of actually doing the project.

For more complex projects it is a good idea to identify critical dates and "milestones" on the timeline.

- Critical dates could be the deadline for a grant for your project. Milestones mark major parts of the project such as completing the plan, getting funding, getting permits, completing construction, and the final unveiling/celebration.

17. DRAWING A PLAN FOR YOUR PROJECT

Visiting and measuring the site is very important. It is also a great learning exercise.

- It will give the participants a much better first-hand experience of the site and a better sense of what is realistic and how things will look and work together.

- They will also have a lot of fun and learn a lot from measuring and drawing a plan of the site.

First give a short lesson on using a tape measure.

- Make sure everyone knows how to read a tape measure. Have them practice measuring some things and make sure they can read the feet and inches correctly. Also make sure they don't mistake "6s" for "9s" and vice versa. This happens a lot.

- It helps to have a long (50' - 100') tape for larger sites. It is easier and more accurate to start at one end with a long tape and measure where each thing is along the entire length of the tape.

- More details on how to measure a site can be found in the Design Basics section.

Make a rough drawing that shows the basic shape of the site. Use this drawing to write down your measurements, where things are, and where you think new things should go.

- You can have the teams report measurements to one person who marks them on the rough plan, or have each team make their own rough plan, depending on how complex the site is.

- You can have the teams report measurements to one person who marks them on the rough plan, or have each team write down the measurements. You should check to make sure the measurements are accurate.

- It's a good idea to have several teams come up with different plans to take back to the drawing board.

- The group can decide which plan is best or combine ideas to make a final plan. (This can be done at a separate meeting when you are back at your program.)

Drawing scale drawings requires technical skill and training, and specialized equipment.

- See the Design Basics section for more information. Go to the library and get a book on how to draw plans if you need more guidance.

- An architect's drawing table with a parallel ruler is very helpful if you can afford it. A simple small portable drawing table with a parallel ruler can be obtained for about $50. A more professional set up will cost about $200.

- Instead of drawing and re-drawing your ideas on the plan, it can be very helpful to make scale cut-outs of the new things you want to include in the site so you can play around with positioning them first.

After drawing a scale plan, it helps to return to the site and mark out in actual size where things should go. You can mark things on the site using chalk, string, or cardboard to get a more realistic idea of how they fit together on the site.

- It is difficult to visualize from a drawn plan how things are really going to be.

- People often try to fit too much into a site. It's important to have enough space between things (especially in playgrounds where there are often code requirements for space).

- If you discover problems, you can revise you plan.

Depending on the complexity of the site and the project, this "activity" will require more than one session.

- At a minimum, there will be one session on site and one session to draw the plans.

- For more complex sites and projects, you may need one session to measure the existing conditions, one session to add the new ideas, one session to evaluate and choose the best ideas, one session to draw the plan, one session to go back to the site and check the plan, and a final session to make any revisions.

It may be useful to get the help of an architect or landscape architect or local building official at this point to advise you of the design requirements for your project.

- There are code requirements for different kinds of places that only professionals know about. For example, swings require a certain amount of space around them.

- You may also want to get community feedback and input.

- For projects with high visibility and impact, it is good to make sure that the immediate community likes your ideas and has an opportunity to give feedback and their own ideas.

18. MAKING A PROJECT WORK PLAN

Decide if you are going to use a short/intensive approach to completing your project or use a more drawn-out approach.

* The short/intensive approach has the advantage of getting big results quickly and generating excitement and enthusiasm. It also requires more people and very careful planning and coordination.

* The drawn-out approach is easier, but often people get bored and frustrated with not seeing results quickly. It is also less efficient because of having to set up and clean up each time you go to the site.

* A compromise is to break larger projects into distinct parts that can be done in several intensive sessions.

A good and detailed project work plan is the key to a successful project.

* The more your group is aware of what needs to be done, the better the project will be.

* Make sure your work plan is realistic. Don't try to do too much in one day.

* Be aware of the best order to do things in and the timing required. For example, take into account the time it takes for paint to dry. (There are quick-drying primer paints that dry in about 20 minutes in dry warm weather.)

* Remember that different age groups have different attention spans. Don't expect people to go for more than one-and-a-half hours without a break. Generally speaking two 1-1/2 hour sessions are about right for a group of youth in the 9-13 age range. It is possible to go for longer periods if there are enough breaks and snacks.

* Don't expect people to necessarily want to stay with one task for too long. People often want variety. Plan your project so people can change tasks.

* You should add details and instructions for complicated tasks so people don't get too confused and need to keep coming to the project supervisor for instructions.

* Make sure you leave enough time at the end for clean up.

* It's a good idea to go over the work plan before the project. Pick team leaders to lead teams of 2-4 people. Each team (or at least the team leaders) should know what they are going to do.

One (or more) person(s) should be chosen to oversee the project.

* This person will be responsible for assuring safety, answering questions, making sure everyone has the materials and tools they need, keeping an eye on

quality, helping with problems, re-assigning tasks when necessary, and keeping track of time.

You can also add a "notes" column to the work plan to make notes of special things to remember.

- For example, under "clean up" you can note that the participants should never touch broken glass, needles, or anything that may be dangerous.

19. DOING THE PROJECT

Make sure all the materials are on site and that "prep" work is done ahead of time.

- Being prepared and ready to get to work helps get people started right away. They will get frustrated and lose interest if they have to wait around for things to be ready.

Safety should be one of your main priorities.

- Always have a complete first aid kit available.

- Any power tool is a potential danger. Make sure anyone who uses a power tool is old enough and is trained in how to use it. Never leave power tools around or plugged in. (They may be a great temptation for younger people.) Hand tools (especially sharp ones) can also be dangerous. They should always be used only for their intended use.

- All power equipment must be grounded, preferably with a ground fault circuit interrupter that will cut the power if there is a short circuit.

- Extreme safety precautions should be taken when working on ladders or staging.

- The basic safety rule is to use common sense. Some other rules are: use safety goggles when using power equipment, hammers, and/or when around dust or debris; always use tools for their intended use; never fool around with tools; use dust masks or respirators when around dust or vapors; use gloves when handling sharp, dirty, or messy things.

- Be sure to check liability issues and any regulations regarding youth and what kind of work they can do.

20. WE COMPLETED THE PROJECT — NOW WHAT?

Going over what was good about the project and what didn't work so well is very important.

- It is important for the youth to immediately celebrate their accomplishment and also to express any frustrations or challenges.

- This can also be very useful in helping future projects work better.

One of the biggest challenges of some projects, especially in urban environments, is maintaining the project. It is also very discouraging to see a project deteriorate.

- Be sure to include maintaining your completed projects in future timelines.

- One of the important lessons in community service is that it takes commitment.

- Adopting a site and keeping it looking good creates pride.

21. CELEBRATIONS AND AWARDS

Celebrations and award-giving are excellent opportunities for youth to learn and practice presenting in public.

- Make sure your group plans and practices for the event so that it is successful.

- Each person should have a role and/or be given the opportunity to say something.

Some businesses and foundations also give awards for projects. (For example a YouthPower project won a Fleet Bank All Stars Award.)

- Do some research to see if your project might be eligible for an award.

22. RECORDING THE PROJECT

Other ways to record your project:

- Make a large poster from photos, quotes, and press clippings of your project. This is a great group project and can be publicly displayed at your program or at events such as celebration/award ceremonies.

- Make a slide show of your project or projects. (You can make good slides from regular photos by taking pictures of them with slide film and special lights for taking slides. Local schools, colleges, and community centers often have this equipment.)

23. GETTING PUBLICITY

It helps to establish a personal relationship with local papers and understand their editorial policies.

* Visit your local press and tell them about your organization and the kinds of projects you do. Ask them what kind of stories they are interested in and the best way to get coverage. Talk to the paper's owner or editor if possible.

* Get to know reporters. Call them directly about stories.

24. YOUNG PEOPLE SPEAK OUT

Evaluation and reflection are very important.

* It is beyond the scope of this manual to give details on the many ways to do evaluation and reflection.

* Try to find materials and guide books on evaluation and reflection.

Vocabulary

The following vocabulary list includes some words used in this manual as well as many you may hear as you talk with people about these projects.

Foam core board: A kind of cardboard with paper on the outside and foam on the inside. It is stiff and light, and can be purchased at art and craft supply stores.

Land use: the activities that land is used for, like houses (called "residential"), shops and offices (called "business" or "commercial"), or parks (called "open space").

Peer leader: a peer leader is an older youth and a participant who acts as a role model and helps to plan and lead meetings.

Project: a project is a short-term activity focused on getting a specific thing done. Examples include cleaning up a park, repainting a building, making a mural.

Plan: (noun) A plan is long-term and more complicated than a project, and provides an overall vision for an area like a neighborhood. To carry out a plan requires working with other groups and doing several projects.

Plan: (verb) To plan involves setting out a series of aims and the steps toward achieving those aims. Both a plan (noun) and a project can be planned (verb).

Site: is a location or a place, usually the location of a project or an activity.

Zoning: a way of dividing up land according to the way it is used. The main zoning categories are: residential, industrial, business or commercial, mixed use, open space, and agriculture.

Treasure chest: further resources

We have used a number of resources in this report. These include (in alphabetical order):

American Architectural Foundation. 1998. Learning by Design Program. http://www.amerarchfoundation.com/srcebook.htm. Accessed April.

This program is run in conjunction with the American Institute of Architects. Each of the 19 AIA regions has a Learning by Design coordinator and there are a variety of useful publications available. For further information contact: Alan R. Sandler, Senior Director, Education Programs, The American Architectural Foundation, 1735 New York, Avenue, NW, Washington, DC 20006.

American Planning Association. 1998. Web page on K-12 education. http://www.planning.org/educ/K-12.html. Accessed March .

This informative section of the APA web site includes general information on the APA's K-12 activities, instructions for requesting free information, lists of K-12 materials available from the APA bookstore, and articles from the APA's "resources" newsletter aimed at K-12 educators. For more information and a free kit of materials contact: APA Education Program, 122 S. Michigan Avenue, Suite 1600, Chicago, IL 60603, call 312-431-9100, or e-mail education@planning.org.

Dunn Foundation. 1996. **Viewfinders: A Visual Environmental Literacy Curriculum**. Warwick, Rhode Island: The Dunn Foundation.

The Dunn Foundation is currently working on a number of projects in environmental education with an emphasis on the appearance of the environment. They can be contacted at 25 Bellows Street, Warwick, Rhode Island 02888 or at http://www.dunnfoundation.org/.

Slafer, Anna, and Kevin Cahill. 1995. **Why Design? Activities and Projects from the National Building Museum**. Chicago: Chicago Review Press.

This 198-page book from the National Building Museum in Washington DC contains 60 exercises and techniques aimed at high school students. Available for $19.95 from the National Building Museum, 401 F Street, NW, Washington, DC 20001.